When *Love* Endures

THE FITZPATRICK FAMILY
SARAH & NICK

judythe morgan

Acknowledgments

The very best critique partners ever: Kim Ford, Stacey Purcell, and Stephanie Wayman. You've pulled me through another Fitzpatrick sibling's story.

Beta Readers: Millie Martin, Tess St. John, Kay Vaccaro for expert reader insights.

And, always my dear husband, who is the role model for all my heroes, my most trusted story editor, and super eagle-eyed copy editor. Love you, always and forever.

Dedication

To my daughter, Sara, who allowed me to model my protagonist Sara (with an H) after her and provided musical details for the manuscript. Her love of music shines.

To my granddaughters, Catherine and Rachel, for letting me use of their names for characters.

The Fitzpatrick Family Of Burton, Texas

Parents

Father:
Colin (Pastor Fitz)
Senior Pastor, New Hope Community

Mother:
Patricia (Ms. Pat)

Children

Matthew, Killed in Afghanistan

Caleb, Burton Police Detective
Wife: Carrie

Sarah, twin of Becca, Music Teacher
Husband: Nick Stephens

Becca, twin of Sarah, School Teacher
Husband: Ethan (Wells) LaMotte

Andy, School Teacher
Wife: Darcy

Josh, Army Sniper
Girlfriend: Mara

Samuel, Missionary

Faith, Law Student

Chapter 1

Growing up, Sarah Fitzpatrick spent hours and hours with her identical twin Becca mapping their lives. Mundane things like what to wear to special events, what honors classes to take, what hairstyle to choose so they looked similar but not carbon copies. Plans for major events like which college to attend and detailed plans for their double wedding to their high school sweethearts, Nick Stephens and Ethan Wells, including names for their children—Carter and Vanessa for her and Nick. Rhett and Scarlett for Becca and Ethan because, you know, her sister would always be the romantic.

Together they created a Twin Protection Society, or TPS for short, to secure their happily-ever-afters. Junior year Becca's plan collapsed when Ethan disappeared. A big black limo arrived and whisked him away. No goodbyes. No calls. No letters. Nada. He simply vanished without a trace.

Senior year, Sarah's Nick broke up with her to marry his former girlfriend, who happened to be pregnant. Exit Nick into the sunset. Sarah hadn't heard from him again and refused to let her heart care.

The TPS plan, so carefully laid out, had totally failed.

Caulking her heart back together, Sarah gave up on marriage. A new plan arose. College. Career. Home. Dating for fun only. No connection. No second date. No blind dates or dating match services. Positively no dating best friends like Ethan and Nick had been.

Life was good. A new TPS plan in full operation with one thing certain—no falling in love again.

Sarah had a job teaching music at the same school as Becca, a home in Burton she co-owned with her twin, and her long-dreamed-of music studio. If a soulmate was out there, God would provide.

As much as Sarah enjoyed teaching music, she disliked Meet the Teacher night every school year almost as much as she dreaded the yearly holiday program, which was fast approaching.

All the parents seemed to want to meet her and promote their child as lead for said production. She'd had a steady stream of suggestions all night. One more session then she could go home and put her feet up.

"Miss Fitzpatrick, Miss Fitzpatrick, he's here." She recognized her new student, Rachel Stephens' voice. The child's cocoa colored, teddy-bear eyes pulled at her heartstrings from the second she'd waltzed into her classroom. The fifth grader had been so worried her father wouldn't be able to attend tonight.

Rachel ran in. "He came like he promised. This is my Dad."

"I'm so happy for you." Sarah smiled at the child then lifted her head to meet the same blue eyes she had once imagined staring into as she said, "I do."

Nick Stephens.

Square jaw, perfect posture, massive shoulders, and piercing eyes. Her Nick had matured into as intriguing a man as he'd been as a teen. Smile wrinkles like deep crow's feet framed the corners of his eyes. He'd always been a great smiler. He flashed one her way now. A warm, friendly, country-boy grin.

The past roared to life and memories squeaked in her head like an orchestra tuning up. Her ears rang until her knees swayed. She sank into the nearest chair.

Ms. Lorene, the streams of gray in her auburn hair flying, huffed through the door. "Sorry. I stopped by Becca's class to give her a hug. We do miss seeing you two at Bible study."

Her familiar face crinkled in concern. The former summer camp nurse, who also happened to be Nick's mom, aimed her hand for Sarah's forehead as if on medic alert. "My dear, you look a little pale. Are you okay?"

Sarah blocked Ms. Lorene's hand and waved her foot in the air. "New shoes. Just resting my feet a little, I'm fine."

Or would be if she could only get her heartbeat under control. *Knees don't fail me now.*

Summoning her best Homecoming Queen smile, she gripped the sides of the chair seat and pushed up. "Glad you could make it."

She'd assumed Nick Stephens still lived in Louisiana and Rachel Marie was just another of the Stephens' kin. Over the years, she'd had several graced her classes. She should have remembered the thing about assumptions.

"Glad to be here." His smile grew. "I wasn't sure. I travel a lot for business and flight schedules can be iffy. That's why we moved in with Mom."

A beat of awkward silence hung between them until Sarah fully processed his words.

He lived here!

"Well, welcome back. I know Rachel's glad you're home." Her voice sounded like an alto trying to sing first soprano.

His mom beamed. "I'm so glad he and Rachel have come home."

What about his wife? Why wasn't she with them? Sarah clamped her lips. Not the time or place to ask. It didn't matter, anyway.

A bell sounded and an announcement that the meet-and-greet had ended blared from the class-room speaker. Sarah led Rachel toward the door.

"Thank you for bringing your father and grand-mother. I'll see you tomorrow." She looked from Nick to his mother. "Nice to see you both again." *Liar, liar pants on fire.*

Lorene took her granddaughter's hand. "Before we go, we were wondering about private lessons. Rachel loves to sing and play around on the piano."

A second bell rang. "That's the last bell. We need to clear the building for the evening. Why don't you give me a call at my studio? We'll talk."

"Thank you." Ms. Lorene walked into the hall, granddaughter in tow.

Nick hung back. "Do you need help stacking chairs, or is that done anymore?"

"Chester gives teachers a break on parent night."

"Chester's still here? Wow! He must be close to a hundred."

"No. We were young. He just seemed old."

"Young but not so smart in hindsight." Nick gave her another bright smile. Her hormones did a little jig in rhythm to her racing pulse.

Still oozing charm. And him a married man. Not working on her. He chose Barb. Without a second thought for Sarah or her feelings.

"Dad, come on. We're gonna leave you," Rachel called from the hallway.

"Coming." He flashed a beguiling half-smile Sarah's way. "You look great. See you around."

He was out the door before Sarah could voice a comeback.

She shook her head. Nick Stephens back in Burton. This was not good. So not good.

Irritation like sand in a shoe followed Sarah to the car then into her house. Becca's car was already in the garage. Sarah tossed her tote into her piano studio and headed into the kitchen, straight to the M&M jar.

"Rough night?" Becca grabbed a handful for herself.

"Ya think?" Sarah reached into the jar. "I dread open house night anyway. Then to discover Rachel Stephens is Nick's daughter. How did I not know that? Did you?"

"Not until I saw him in the hallway between sessions. I would have texted, but a parent waylaid me. We're never going to know what's going on around town now that we can't get to Wednesday morning Bible study."

"True." Sarah circled her fingers around the back of her neck and kneaded. "I was blown away when Rachel walked in with him. I thought she was one of the cousins."

"Me, too." Becca placed her hand over her heart. "My, he's still a looker, isn't he?"

"Pfffft! I didn't notice."

Becca chuckled. "Right. That's why you're stuffing down all the M&M's."

Having a twin is such a pain sometimes. She reads my mind.

"Okay maybe he did look good in a more mature way. But there's still Barb. She wasn't with them. Wonder why. I think I'll call Mom, see what she knows."

"Put her on speaker."

Sarah pulled her cell from her pocket and scrolled for her mom's number. "Mom, Sarah. Quick question. I know it's late. Why is Nick Stephens in town?"

"Becca here. You're on speaker."

"Hi, Becca. I'm not sure, Sarah. Someone at Bible study mentioned they'd seen him. Probably should have called to tell you. I got busy and forgot. Sorry."

"No problem. I was just wondering what his story was. Do you know?"

"Wish I could help you out. Lorene came in late for Bible study and left without hanging around to visit. I didn't get to ask her." Mom paused a beat. "Are you okay with him being back?"

Becca leaned in. "His daughter's in her music class. She has no choice."

"It'll probably be awkward at first, but you're both adults now. You'll handle it. What happened in the past is the past."

Sarah clenched her back teeth. She didn't share her mom's glass half-full outlook. "I don't know. On top of having her in class, Ms. Lorene asked about piano lessons."

"You can do this, Sarah. Talk with Lorene. She'll fill you in about what's going on."

"I guess. Thanks." Sarah tried to keep the whine

out of her voice. She didn't need Nick Stephens around messing in her world again. He'd crushed her heart once. She couldn't, no wouldn't, let it happen again. "See you Sunday, Mom."

Becca pinned Sarah with a teacher's hard look. "You're going to say no to Rachel taking lessons, aren't you?"

Another twin mindread bullseye. Sarah gathered a handful of M&Ms. "I'm not sure I can fit in another student. I only have so much time after school."

"Sarah, you know you'd fit anyone else in. Don't punish the daughter because her father jilted you in high school. You're bigger than that."

"Am I? Better to just say no. Keep things simple." She shrugged and popped the M&Ms into her mouth.

Becca put her hand over the top of the jar. "Don't be that way. Besides, it sounds like Ms. Lorene would be the one you deal with anyway."

"What if it's not? What if Nick brings her to lessons? Or Barb? I'm not sure I can be that gracious."

"Yes, you can. Think about Rachel." Becca screwed the lid back on the M&M jar and put it away.

Rachel's soft brown eyes flashed in Sarah's head. All arguments died on her lips. "Okay, okay."

Chapter 2

Nick scooted one of his daughter's stuffed animals toward her to make room for their nightly bedtime story. Their therapist assured him Rachel's renewed attachment to her security blanket zoo would eventually wane once she felt more comfortable in her new situation. He hoped so with all her *lovies* tucked in around her, there was hardly room for her in the bed, much less him.

A fruity scent from some shampoo she'd seen advertised and talked her granny into buying clouded the air. He missed the clean smell of the baby stuff. His little girl was growing up too fast.

After one chapter of her Harriet the Spy mystery book, he kissed her still damp hair. "Sweet dreams."

"One more chapter."

"It's late. Way past your bedtime."

Her lip protruded in an exaggerated pout. "Tomorrow's Saturday. I can sleep in. I need to know if Harriet finds another clue."

"Sweet pea…" Sleeping in had never been his daughter's thing.

"Pretty please." She tilted her head and fluttered her thick lashes. A technique she'd watched her mother use. Rachel would be a handful when she started thinking about boys as more than pals.

"Just one."

He firmly closed the book when he finished that chapter and set it on the bedside table. Pulling the covers up, he kissed Rachel's forehead. "See you tomorrow."

"For sure?" The anxiety in her two words tugged on his heart. That wasn't Barb-learned. That was because of all that had happened.

"For sure." He promised and gave her another goodnight hug. "Nighty night."

His cell vibrated as he closed his daughter's door. He smiled seeing the caller ID. "Hey there."

"Have you seen her?" His best friend, and now partner, sounded like he was in the next room, not France.

"I have."

"And?"

"Becca's just as beautiful as she was in high school. So's Sarah."

Air from a heavy sigh gushed through the phone. "How could we have been so stupid?"

Nick gave a soft chuckle. "Rachel would say it's because we're boys."

"So young and so wise. Like my little sister, Genevieve. How's she doing?"

"Still clingy, but her new therapist said to expect that. Believe it or not, our therapist is Mara Burke, remember her? She's got a practice here now. Says I should be patient. Give Rachel time to adjust."

But time wouldn't erase the guilt he carried like a ball and chain. Seeing Sarah tonight only added another link to the already heavy shackles.

"Listen to her. You're on the right track again. Patience, my friend, patience."

"I hear you. First thing Monday I'm looking for office space. I'll keep you posted."

"Perfect. Go sleep off your jetlag. Talk to you soon."

Ethan knew about patience. So did Nick. They were both finally at a place in their lives where they could fight to win Sarah and Becca back. But, with their past actions hanging over them, winning the twins over would be a major challenge.

Nick jackknifed upright when he saw the time on his cell. He never slept this late. No telling what his mischievous daughter had gotten into. Visions of the last glitter glue episode danced in his head. "Rachel?"

He swung his feet to the floor. "Rachel Marie, what are you doing?"

His mom appeared in the doorway, jogging his memory. Relief washed through his body.

"She's not here. I thought you needed some extra rest after your long travel day yesterday and the time change from Paris. I let her go to her new friend, Catherine's."

Already his mom had a better handle on his daughter than he'd been able to muster since Barb died. "Thank you."

"Join me in the kitchen when you're ready. Fresh pot of coffee's brewing."

Minutes later, the familiar scents of yeast and coffee brewing greeted Nick when he walked into the kitchen. A glance around revealed bread rising on the stove. A basket of biscuits on the table. His mom, baker extraordinaire.

The kitchen timer dinged. She pulled a sheet of cookies from the oven and slid them onto the cooling rack.

Another scent of childhood hit him. "Chocolate chip?"

"Of course, Rachel's favorite. Like father, like daughter."

Pride puffed his chest. He lifted the cookie she offered from the spatula. "She is, isn't she?"

His mom raised an egg in the air. "Fried or scrambled?"

"Fried." He'd missed sweet tea and fried food on his trip to France. Who would've believed Foie Gras and French wine got old?

She stretched bacon across the iron skillet. "So, what are you about today? It's Saturday, you know. You and your Dad always went fishing on Saturdays. Ethan tagged along most of the time. I think Sarah went a time or two."

Nick nodded. "Yeah. Good times." But that was a lifetime ago. "When's Rachel due home?"

"I'm planning to pick her up and take her shopping with me. Been teaching her how to spot a deal."

He'd learned more about ROI—return on investment—in the grocery store with his mom than he had in all his business classes. "How's she liking that?"

"Seems to be catching on. Head for figures, same as you."

"What if I pick her up? We can do the shopping. Give you a break and us some time together."

Lorene placed his breakfast plate in front of him, dropped her arm around his shoulder, and gave a squeeze. "That'd be terrific. I'll get the list together."

"And the address for Rachel's friend," he mumbled around a mouthful of egg.

"Right." She pulled out the chair across from him.

Nick braced himself. His mom only sat when she had something that demanded his undivided attention.

"How was it seeing Sarah last night?" Not one to beat around the bush, his mom.

His throat clogged up, like he'd swallowed a cotton ball. When he didn't answer, she pinned him with a stare over her coffee mug. "Time you started to think about the future. You're way too young to spend the rest of your life single."

Seemed easy when she said it like that. It was

never that easy. He pushed his eggs around his plate. "You saw. Sarah didn't seem overly excited to see me. That ship's sailed."

"She hasn't married. According to Ms. Pat, neither twin even dates."

Hope kicked him in the chest.

Sarah headed for the zucchini in the produce department, but quickly executed a sharp U-turn when she spotted Rachel and her dad examining a cantaloupe.

A little voice called after her. "Look, it's Miss Fitzpatrick!"

Why were students always so excited to see their teacher outside the classroom? Did they really think she lived at the school 24/7? She gave a little wave and continued her retreat.

A man in a store scooter blocked her escape. Stuck, she surveyed other routes to reach the zucchini. All paths led by Nick and Rachel. Argh!

This was exactly the problem with him moving back to town. Wasn't enough she'd dreamed about him for years, now he was live and in living color right in front of her face. Standing between her and a simple zucchini with that heartrending smile.

She swiveled her cart around. "Hi, Rachel. Did you find a good cantaloupe?"

Dumb question! Did anyone ever know if those things were good until it was sliced? Nick Stephens was so messing with her head.

"Granny says the good ones have no green on the outside. When you scratch and sniff, it's supposed to smell sweet. I'm teaching Dad." She raised the melon to Sarah's nose.

Smelled like a cantaloupe rind to Sarah. "I'll have to remember that."

"I never realized there was so much to learn about cantaloupe buying." Nick, his face deadpan, put the melon into their cart. Another of his gifts, the ability to hold back a grin.

Sarah addressed Rachel. "Any tips on buying zucchini? I'm picking some up for a cake I'm baking for tomorrow's potluck after church."

Rachel's face scrunched like she'd bit into a sour grape. "A cake made with vegetables. That doesn't sound very good."

Nick gave an exaggerated sigh. "Wrong. It's yummy. I love it."

Rachel swiveled her attention to her dad. "Can we stay for potluck after church?"

"For a slice of Sarah's chocolate chip zucchini cake? Definitely."

Today the produce aisle. Tomorrow the church aisle.

Sarah wanted to bite her tongue off. Why'd she bring up the potluck?

Chapter 3

Sure enough, next morning at church Sarah sensed Nick's eyes on her. She peeked over the top of her choir folder. There he was. Rachel on one side. Ms. Lorene on the other. Still no Barb. Were they divorced?

He caught her looking and winked. Just like that they were back in high school playing peek-a boo.

Oh no you don't mister. No fun and games with you.

All she needed to do was get her eyes to cooperate. She whipped her attention back to the choir director.

After the service, Sarah got trapped in the kitchen serving food. When she finally filled her plate, Becca motioned her over to the places she'd saved. Two full plates sat across from them. "They've gone to get dessert before the good stuff is gone."

She recognized Nick's tie beside one of the plates. Her jaw clicked as she clamped her back teeth. She shot her best *I'm-going-to-kill-you* glare at her sister. "Nick? You pick a place across from Nick!"

Becca threw her hands up in defense. "Not on purpose. It's crowded. There wasn't any place else. You don't have to sit here. You can always go stand at the kitchen counter with Mom and her friends."

"Funny." Last time Sarah had done that she'd been trapped into grandbaby talk and questions about whether she planned to give her mom any.

Some choice. Hot coals or the boiling pot? She dropped her plate to the table with a thud.

Rachel arrived with two dessert plates. One with Sarah's zucchini cake. The other piled with chocolate chip cookies. "I'm only tasting the vegetable cake. I probably won't like it. No matter what Dad says."

Nick's tongue slid around his lips. "I hope you don't. I'll be happy to take it."

Shaking her head, Becca pointed to the two huge pieces on his plate. "Don't you think you got enough?"

"Couldn't help myself. It's been forever since I had some." His gaze connected with Sarah's. "I've missed it."

The double entendre flamed her cheeks.

"You won't be sorry. She still wins a blue ribbon at the county fair."

Sarah elbowed her sister. *TMI.*

"Ah, the fair. We had some good times there. I'll have to take Rachel next year."

"Your wife should join you. I'm sure she'd enjoy it." The snippy dig was out before Sarah could stop it.

Becca kicked her shin. Sarah grimaced. *The man absolutely kills my filters, and my manners.*

"She can't. She's in heaven." Rachel's voice so filled with sadness only her lips formed the words.

Sarah's fork sank to her plate. *Barb's dead.* Too stunned to get much air behind them, her words came out like a squeaky violin. "I'm so sorry. I… we… I didn't know."

"It was unexpected, but we're managing." Shadows flashed in his eyes, then just as quickly disappeared. He patted his daughter's hand and took another bite of cake. "Your cake is as delicious as I remember."

Unexpected? That raised more questions in Sarah's head. Before she could speak, Becca slid her hand under the table and squeezed Sarah's knee with a don't-you-dare.

Thank heavens for twin mindreading and TPS. No questions. No involvement. Just let it go.

The pageant smile slipped into place. "Thank you," she muttered.

Sarah escaped the potluck as fast as she could—before her mouth betrayed her again. At home, she went straight for the comfort of M&Ms, snarfing down a huge handful.

She'd loathed Nick Stephens since he jilted her in high school. She thought she was over him. The door on the most heartbreaking, humiliating moment of her life slammed shut. Finished.

Another fistful of candy went into her mouth. Obviously not. Like the jealous teen she'd once been, she'd taken a poke at the man she hadn't seen in over a decade about his dead wife.

She sighed inwardly. Made sense feelings would linger. Nick had been her first love. No one else would ever measure up. More M&Ms.

When she arrived home, Becca found her hugging the nearly empty jar and jerked the container from her grip. "You're going to make yourself sick. And fat."

"It's what I deserve. Me and my runaway mouth." She dropped her head against the back of the couch in defeat.

"You didn't know Barb died. Your little dig backfired. You apologized. Get over it."

Get over it? He'd be orbiting her world. A single dad. How would her traitorous heart survive?

"Did you see Rachel's face?"

"I did." Becca nodded. "She misses her mother. Wouldn't you?"

"Of course, I'd miss Mom."

"You need to call Ms. Lorene and set up piano lessons for Rachel."

"I'm not sure teaching piano to Nick Stephens' daughter is such a good idea. Especially now that I know he's a widower. Better to avoid him altogether."

Her cell rang. "Hello."

"Sarah, it's Lorene Stephens. Your mom gave me your number. Is this a good time to talk about lessons for Rachel?"

This was either a God-eavesdropping thing or her mom-and-sister-in-cahoots-playing-cupid thing. Sarah suspected the latter.

"Hi, Ms. Lorene." She shot eye darts at Becca and headed to her schedule calendar in the music studio. "Now's good."

Sarah peered out her studio window the next week and saw Ms. Lorene walking up the sidewalk with Rachel. Her whole body relaxed.

She opened the front door before Ms. Lorene knocked. "Hi. You ready to get started, Rachel?"

Ms. Lorene's hand rested on Rachel's shoulder. "I'm going to run some errands. What time should I be back?"

"We'll probably run overtime, this being the first lesson. Be back in say, forty-five minutes."

Excited, Rachel headed for the piano. Her smile broad. Her swinging feet barely reached the floor. Sarah knew she was going on eleven, but from her size she could pass for much younger.

"Let's use this so your feet reach." Sarah slid the small step stool she used for younger students under the girl's feet. "Why don't we start with scales?"

Rachel lifted her hands, wrists raised and straight, fingers curved in perfect position above middle C, and executed a perfect C scale arpeggio ending with the I, IV, V7 chords in a flourish. She shifted to the key of C#, moved to D, and so on all the way to B Major.

Sarah applauded. "That was fabulous. Have you had lessons?"

"Nah, Mom didn't have time to take me like Granny. I've been teaching myself. Wanna hear?" She played a medley of familiar church hymns.

"That was wonderful." She placed a beginner book on the music stand. "Let's see what you can do with this?"

Rachel looked at her. "I can't exactly read all the notes. If you play it for me..."

O-kay. "No worries, that's why I'm here."

By the end of the lesson, Rachel could match all the notes in the treble clef, and bass, to the keyboard and play through the entire book of level one lessons.

Wowzer! A child prodigy? Definitely gifted. Did Nick and her grandmother know?

Ms. Lorene tapped on the studio door. "How'd it go?"

Sarah motioned her inside. Nick stepped around his mother.

Sarah froze. In her excitement over Rachel's talent, remembering who her father was had slipped from her head. Now he was back before her eyes. Flesh and blood. How could she have forgotten?

"I want to talk to you and Ms. Lorene. Rachel, there's a jar of M&Ms on the kitchen counter. Go get yourself some while we visit a minute."

"But I want to hear what you say."

"It's all about schedules and stuff. You'd be bored."

Sarah handed her a theory book. "You can look over some of these lessons in the next book if you want."

Rachel took the book from Sarah, looked to her granny and dad. "M&Ms okay?"

"Just a few. Don't want to spoil your supper," Ms. Lorene cautioned.

"What Granny said." Nick turned his attention to Sarah. His brow furrowed. "Is there a problem?"

Sarah reached out to touch his arm and wipe the concern from his face. Halfway through the motion, she realized that was the stupidest idea ever. *Do not slip into old habits with him.* She tucked her hair behind her ears instead.

"Not at all. The opposite. Rachel is extremely talented. I hope you have a good piano."

Ms. Lorene shoulders rose in a wince. "Mine's kinda old and not holding a tune so well anymore. Rachel complains whenever she plays on it."

Nick stuffed his hands in his pocket. "We were hoping you'd go piano shopping with us. Neither of us knows the first thing about a quality piano."

Sarah stared at him, suddenly understanding what a deer spotlighted in oncoming headlights must feel like. No way to avoid the impact.

She could send him a link for a piano she recommended. But a talented child deserved the best piano to advance her potential, and every acoustic piano had a different feel. A different tone. Unless Nick had experienced a remarkable transformation, he'd never know the difference. He'd focus only on the price tag. Sarah couldn't let that happen.

Nick's voice drew her back. "We'd go whenever it's convenient for you. Mom's piano will do until then."

"I could take her to the church to practice," Lorene suggested.

A mixture of compassion and frustration shuffled through Sarah. Neither was a satisfactory solution. Only someone tone deaf could live with an out-of-tune instrument. Rachel's perfect pitch ear would scream. And, people were always milling around in the church. There'd never be a quiet time for her to concentrate. Rachel deserved better than an out-of-tune piano.

Rachel appeared at Nick's side. Her eyes, a blend of plea and demand, peered up at Sarah. "You have to come. We won't get the perfect piano if you don't."

Ever since Nick Stephens showed up, her life felt a little like walking on quicksand. He was everywhere. Sucking her in.

But it wasn't the child's fault who her father is.

"Sure," she said in her best pageant tone and lifted her cheek in another smile.

Chapter 4

Every evening when he came in from the office, Rachel greeted Nick with "Did you call Miss Sarah?" There'd been no time with all the unending LaMotte Wells Services' due diligence talks and negotiations about their oil companies' merger. He and Ethan considered their handshake a done deal on the partnership. Ethan's grand-père didn't.

Nick could have carved out a few minutes to talk to Sarah, except he'd gotten the impression she wasn't all that excited about spending time with him. Truth was, he was scared she'd blow him off forever. That would be death to his plans.

Today, he was determined to pin her to a specific date for piano shopping and have a yes answer for his daughter's question when she asked.

Walking to his truck after a meeting that felt like nine rounds with the boxer Saul 'Canelo' Alvarez, Nick searched Sarah's name in his phone contacts. His call went straight to voice mail.

Frustration rumbled in his chest. *Be positive.* Maybe she wasn't avoiding him but had a student and couldn't talk.

He waited for the beep. "Sarah, this is Nick...Nick Stephens." He shook his head. Why was he using his last name? Hopefully there wasn't another Nick in her life. But would she recognize the sound of his voice? The years never wiped away her familiar sound for him.

"Would Saturday work to go piano shopping? Rachel is so eager..." He cleared his throat. "Right, so can you please call so we can set something up?"

Lame. He sounded like a nervous teenager asking for a first date. He climbed in the truck and headed toward the freeway.

His cell rang on the way home. He switched on the truck's Bluetooth. "Nick Stephens."

"Hi, Nick. This is Sarah. Saturday works. Have you decided what kind of piano you want?"

"Not yet. I know nothing about pianos except they have eighty-eight keys and Rachel makes them all sing."

Sarah laughed. "That she does. Basically, there are uprights and grands."

"I know what grands are. What's an upright?"

"Uprights are what the name implies. Sounding boards go up. Models come in spinets, consoles, and studio. All with different sounds and looks. You need to do some homework to decide which you want."

A new strategy formed in his head. The perfect, non-threatening way to spend solo time with Sarah. *Keep it cool and light.*

"It does sound like there's a lot I need to know before we shop. Let's grab a quick dinner. You can tutor me. I hate shopping clueless."

Silence echoed in his ear. He waited while a bundle of nerves bounced in his gut like a cat on a hot tin roof. His finger tapped the steering wheel as the silence lengthened. "Sarah, you still there?"

"Yes."

"I'm in the truck on my way home. I was afraid I'd lost you. So, what do you say? Okay to swing by and pick you up?" Counting on a yes, he took the freeway exit then turned toward her house.

"Won't Rachel be expecting you?" Her question broadcast her reluctance.

"She has a friend over. She won't miss me...and I won't miss the giggling, girlie antics." Last sleepover he'd ended up with neon pink toenails, which Rachel checked the next morning to be sure he hadn't removed the polish after she went to bed.

"Okay. Where? I'll meet you."

"Not necessary. Umm, I'm out front. I'll call Mom and let her know. Come on out when you're ready."

The blinds split and Sarah peered out. He recognized that face. *Oops.* Maybe he shouldn't have presumed.

Replays of long-ago times when she would refuse to come out to talk to him tumbled from his memory vault. Stupid arguments and his even stupider actions that ended up costing him the girl who still claimed his heart. He'd made such a mess of things marrying Barb, except for Rachel. She was worth all the drama and strife Barb had dished out.

He was not going to botch things with Sarah this time. Sliding from his truck, he hustled to her door.

Sarah watched Nick's long-legged gait eat up her sidewalk. The sight transported her to the first time her heart had seen him. Not her eyes, but her heart.

He'd been in her world forever, then one day on a bus ride home from a youth group trip, he'd kissed her. A silly, closed-lip, hard mouthed bump of a first kiss. After that, he was in her every waking thought. Every daydream and every fantasy of her future.

Until Barb. And forever vanished in smoke like a genie disappearing back into his jar. She'd locked Nick, and those happy days away. Hadn't thought much about him in years.

Not much? Don't lie to yourself. It's been a lot more than much lately.

She gave her head a shake and studied his approaching face. Faint lines bracketed his mouth telling her life might not have given him what he'd expected either. He was still devastatingly handsome. *Don't go there.*

She opened the door "Nick. I—"

His lips curved in the penitent half-smile he'd perfected. "I didn't mean to presume. If you want to meet some place, just say where. I'll follow in my truck."

She hesitated. Part of her wanted to meet him some place. Slow things down. Her practical self recognized how silly it was to take two cars to the same place. She blew away her annoyance. "It's fine. Let me grab the information I printed out for you."

I'm doing this for Rachel. Having a good piano will help her.

Ha! Lying to yourself again?

Okay. Spending time with her dad is a nice fringe benefit.

She stepped on the running board to slid inside. His hand supported her elbow. Her pulse stumbled at his touch.

He rounded the hood and climbed in beside her. "Feelin' Good Café work?"

Their old go-to place. Did she really need those memories?

On the other hand, he'd only just returned to Burton. He probably didn't know any other place. "There's also a new Italian place."

"I hear that's a bit fancy. Let's save it for another time."

Another time? The hairs on her neck bristled. "Nick—"

He held up a hand to stall her rebuff. "Let's see how tonight goes. Then we'll decide about more."

Sarah closed her eyes. She was *so* in trouble.

After the waitress took their orders, Sarah spread the printouts of piano models across the table. Nick shifted his chair closer. His scent circled her in a cocoon of memories of other times they'd sat side-by-side at this very table. They'd been so young, so hopeful. So full of dreams.

But they were no longer those people.

She pointed to one of the pictures. "This is an upright. It will give the sound closest to a grand."

Nick laid his hand over hers. "Before we get into pianos. I need to ask you to do something for me."

Even the slight touch sent long-buried emotions, memories she'd never be able to bury deep enough, to the surface. Sarah reached for her water, swallowed a mouthful, hoping to get past the myriad of emotions, thoughts, and questions zigzagging inside her head. "What do you mean?"

"Rachel has no idea about our history. I told her we were classmates. But I don't want her to know about the other. Yet."

Did he actually think she'd want to share what had happened with his daughter? Living through the debacle of being the jilted girlfriend had been hard enough. "Okay. Fine by me."

"You think you can convince your family to go along? Rachel's dealing with a lot. Learning I married her mother because I had to won't help anyone."

Sarah understood how he'd want to spare Rachel, who was the innocent bystander. She met his gaze and thought she saw a silent apology for causing her pain. "I'll talk to them."

"Thank you." He squeezed her hand. "I hated the way things happened. If you'll let me, I want a second chance."

"No. Don't go there. I'm your daughter's teacher. We can be friends, but anything else is long gone. Done. Finished."

"Not if I can change your mind."

Sarah jerked her hand away. She wasn't going there.

The crestfallen look on his face took her back to the night he'd told her he was marrying Barb. That night he'd looked like a drowned kitten as he spoke. But tonight, there was a twinkle of hopeful determination in his voice. She shook her head slowly then flipped to the next page of her notes, explained the pros and cons of each model, ending with the spinet. "It's the smallest piano and sometimes hard to regulate. That's what your mother has."

"What kind do you have?"

"An upright. Someone gifted the church a baby grand. The board voted to give the old one to me when Becca and I bought our house."

"Very generous. Bet your Dad had a hand in that."

"Nope, it was Becca. We watch out for one another."

He gave a knowing nod. "I remember the Twin Protection Society. 'Bout drove me and Ethan crazy. So, you and Becca still use that?"

"We do. Comes in handy at times."

The waitress arrived with their food.

They both reached to clear room for the plates. His bare forearm above the crisp white sleeves rolled halfway up his arm brushed hers. A quiver of electricity shot between them. Oxygen stalled somewhere between her nose and lungs. She could have sworn she heard his breath catch. Their gazes locked.

"Okay if I take these home to study?" His words whistled like they'd come through a tunnel.

The waitress cleared her throat, breaking the spell, and set their dinners down.

Oh geez, what am I doing? Sarah tapped the pages together and handed them to him. "Sure. That's why I printed them."

"Y'all need anything else, just holler." She headed to the kitchen.

Awkward beats passed before they focused on their meals with small talk punctuated with reminisces until Sarah could stand it no longer. She wanted answers. "Why'd you come back here?"

Nick swallowed. She watched his Adam's apple slide up and down. "I had an opportunity for a business partnership with an old friend. But mostly for Rachel. I tried on my own for a year after Barb died. It wasn't working."

He stared into his plate for several long seconds as if debating with himself before he continued, "Rachel needed a mom's touch. Mom offered to come live with us. But we needed a fresh start away from all the bad memories, so here we are."

"Rachel must have been very close to her mother." Sarah couldn't bring herself to say Barb's name.

"No. It wasn't that so much. It was how she died. Rachel was alone with her when Barb collapsed." He picked at the remains on his plate. "I was on a rig in the Gulf. Took me a few days to get home."

"I'm so sorry, Nick. How awful for her. For both of you." Sarah knew she shouldn't ask, but she had to know the rest. Ms. Lorene had never mentioned Barb died. "What happened?"

The grief in his eyes was so heavy. She clasped her hands under the table so she wouldn't hold his hand.

"Autopsy revealed a cerebral aneurysm. They'd been at the park. Barb told Rachel she had a headache and wanted to go home to lie down. They started back, but Barb collapsed. Rachel called 911. Because I wasn't there, one of the EMTs stayed with her until CPS arrived."

He pinched the bridge of his nose. "I should have been there. I wasn't. Rachel spent the worst night of her life with strangers."

Without hesitation, Sarah covered his forearm with her hand. "That must have been so hard."

Nick signaled for the check, dropped his other hand over hers, squeezed softly. "It eats at me. All. The. Time."

Sarah forced the other million questions aside for now.

When they arrived at her house, he patted the printouts on the console between them. "Thanks for this. I'll discuss the options with Mom and Rachel." He came around to her door and offered his hand. "We'll have a decision by Saturday."

"That's great. Call if you have any questions." *Jeez Louise.* Had she really just encouraged him to call? Where was Becca and the TPS when she needed them?

"Will do." He started to walk away then turned back. "How about having breakfast with us before we head to the piano store?"

Despite herself, Sarah nodded. "Eight-thirty? The store opens at ten. We'd have plenty of time."

"Perfect. It was good to spend time with you, Sarah. I've missed you." His lips brushed her cheek. He shrugged like he wanted to fake nonchalance at what must have been the stunned expression on her face. "Another chance, that's all I'm asking."

Sarah dashed inside, rested her forehead against the closed door. He was so slipping under her TPS plan's radar.

Becca's hand touched her on the shoulder. "Everything okay?"

She twirled around sure her twin could hear her heart beating like a snare drum. "Nick's happening again."

Chapter 5

Rachel jumped at Sarah's suggestion of the local Pancake House for breakfast when they picked her up on Saturday.

Nick disguised his groan, not wanting to squelch their enthusiasm. The place was a sticky vat. Every single time he took Rachel, without fail, he came away with gooey syrup on him somewhere.

But, in the end, he'd said yes for more time with his daughter and the woman he still loved. Hoping to prevent another sticky incident, he slid into the booth beside his daughter.

After their pancakes arrived, they all went for the syrup containers at the same time. A terrible mix of hands and tilting pitchers could only end one way. Sadly, sitting beside Rachel meant his timing and reach were off. Syrup went everywhere, coating the table, Rachel's hand, Sarah's hand and his.

"Oops." Sarah dropped her napkin onto the oozing river of blueberry before the stream cascaded over the edge of the table.

Nick waved for the waitress, who dashed over with a wet cloth.

She flashed a sympathetic smile. "It happens. No worries."

Sarah slid from the booth and extended her un-syrupy hand to Rachel. "Let's go clean up. We don't want sticky hands while we're testing out pianos."

Nick followed their retreat thinking what a natural mother Sarah would be. Same scenario with Barb would have erupted into screaming. Once she'd slapped Rachel when his daughter came home from school with paint on her dress. He willed the hurtful old memory away.

The rest of breakfast was uneventful, the drive into Houston pleasant, and the piano store so much larger than he'd imagined. As far as his eye could see, nothing but pianos. Nick was glad he had Sarah to help him make an intelligent decision.

Rachel's eyes swept the place. She headed straight for the ten-foot grand in the center of the showroom.

All was good...until, after over an hour of Mozart and chopsticks on dozens of pianos, Nick asked Sarah for her recommendation.

"An upright like mine," she answered.

"But I want a baby grand." Rachel stomped her foot. "You promised."

Sarah whipped a frown his way. "You promised?"

"No, I said we'd look at baby grands."

Rachel was not giving up. "That's the same as promising."

"Even if a grand would fit, and I don't think it will, it will overpower your granny's living room," Sarah said. "An upright gives almost the same sound, is smaller, and much more practical."

"A grand will so fit. Granny and I measured," Rachel argued.

Nick shrugged. "It does."

"See." Rachel's narrowed eyes screamed told-you-so at Sarah.

Before the discussion turned ugly, Nick started toward the salesman who had been working with them. "Let's see what I can negotiate."

Sarah placed her hand on his arm. Incredulousness clouded her face. "Wait. An upright will give a great sound and be far more practical for your mom's house."

"But Dad said we aren't always gonna live at Granny's." Rachel gaze bored into his. "One of these days we'll have our own house, and I'll have a new Mommy who likes music as much as I do. That's what you promised."

Sarah shifted a startled look his way. "Oh, really?"

"Fantasy bedtime story," Nick lipped.

"Rachel, just try the upright one more time while your dad and I talk." Sarah gave a school-teacher head tilt indicating Nick should come with her.

Busted. His daughter's innocent comment may have cost him ground he thought he was gaining. He inhaled deeply and followed.

Sarah whirled to face him once they were beyond Rachel's hearing. "What are you thinking?"

"Maybe I shouldn't be feeding Rachel's fantasy."

"As long as you recognize it's fantasy. But that's not what I meant. Are you seriously going to buy a baby grand for a ten-year-old who could very likely decide tomorrow she wants to be a world class gymnast?"

He stifled his sigh of relief. Justifying a baby grand for his daughter would be a slam dunk compared to defending his fantasy of a life together for them.

In the background, Rachel played some tune she'd been practicing. He tilted his head in that direction. "Okay, but uhm, the song she's playing did sound better on the small grand."

"It does. But it's a lot of money to spend on a fascination she may outgrow."

"Not my Rachel. All she's ever wanted was to play a baby grand piano. Same as you. Barb was the problem."

Confusion marred Sarah's pretty face. "What do you mean?"

"Rachel's constant playing and composing got on her nerves. Barb called it banging and never found time to take her for lessons. When I was out on a rig, she gave away the piano. Rachel didn't come out of her room for a week."

Sarah's mouth formed a perfect *O* of astonishment. "That's horrible. Rachel deserves to explore her talent." She started to say something else, instead took a step back before she spoke again. "It doesn't sound like your past was what you wanted but you should think about what you're doing here. What's your mom going to do with everything she has to move out to fit that baby grand?"

"First of all, like Rachel said, we're not going to live with Mom forever." He winked at her. "Rachel's fairytale and my mine are the same. I'm sorry I hurt you, Sarah, and I'm not giving up hope of getting back together." *You are the keystone to our fairytale.*

Seconds of silence followed, tiny ticks of time as the meaning in his words sank in. He watched the storm of emotions play across her face. The doubt. The hurt. The pain. All caused by his stupid actions.

"Don't go there, Nick. Please."

He swallowed the sucker punch he deserved, knowing he wasn't giving up. "I won't. For now." He raised his hand to touch her cheek but thought better and returned the conversation to his daughter. "But Rachel is determined about a baby grand. Her mind was made up before we got here."

Sarah's shoulders relaxed, telling him he'd been right move. "There's still the big price difference."

"Price isn't an issue, working on rigs all those years paid well. I've got a healthy savings. A grand is what Rachel's always wanted. No reason she shouldn't have it."

Sarah rolled her eyes and shook her head slowly. "I give up. Every little girl should be so lucky."

With details on delivery worked out, Rachel led them back to the truck with a million-watt smile on her face. Her steps bouncy. Before she hopped inside, she gave him a hug. "I love you. Thank you. Thank you."

"You're welcome. Now there's no reason for you not to ace a Juilliard audition and save me thousands of tuition dollars."

Both girls laughed at his lame joke. Sarah's hair moved gently as a breeze blew, and Nick decided to push his luck further. "Shall we celebrate over lunch?"

He lifted Rachel into the truck's backseat then opened Sarah's door. "That okay with you?"

"Sounds terrific as long as it's not Pancake House." Sarah flashed a teasing grin to Rachel.

"I'm sorry. It was an accident. I didn't mean to spill syrup."

"We know. But I think avoiding syrup for lunch is a great idea." Nick rounded the truck and climbed in. His step had the same bounce as his daughter's had.

He was going to win Sarah Fitzpatrick's heart again.

Three days later, Sarah's car pulled into his mom's driveway.

"She's here. She's here." Rachel raced out the front door, grabbed Sarah's hand, and pulled her inside. "You're gonna love it as much as I do."

Rachel swept her hand like Vanna White toward the baby grand piano in Ms. Lorene's living room. "Ta da. I told you it'd fit."

Sarah stroked the keys like a mother would her newborn's head. "You okay with losing half your living room, Ms. Lorene?"

"I love it. I don't play as well as either of you, but I do love plunking around. Why don't you play something for us, Sarah?"

"I will." Rachel sat on the concert bench and proceeded to play her rendition of a hymn from memory.

Nick placed his hand on Rachel's shoulders. "Granny meant Sarah. We haven't heard her play anything in a very long time. Let's let her try it out."

Before Barb happened, he'd listened to Sarah practice for music guild juries, competitions, and attended many of her performances. She'd been amazing to watch. He lifted Rachel off the bench. "You can sit with me."

He executed a perfect butler bow and waved Sarah toward the piano. She hesitated until the pull of the beautiful instrument finally won. She settled at the keyboard, adjusted the concert bench, and, with a soft smile aimed at him, she lifted her hands into position. The sound of Für Elise filled the room.

"I remember this one. Beethoven," he said after the first seconds. She'd played the piece in her first music guild competition and practiced so often he felt like he could have played it himself.

Time blurred between past and present as he watched. Her back was straight as she swayed back and forth, side to side with the music. He could tell each note floated through her body as she lost herself to the beautiful composition that had earned her the highest Guild rating.

After the last note, she swiveled around. Her gaze met Rachel's. "That was my first-ever piece for Guild and still one of my favorites. I think it's one you could master."

Rachel, who had been in a trance as Sarah played, smiled. "I could. Play some more."

"It's your turn, Nick. Come join me. We'll play our favorite duet."

Nick flipped imaginary tuxedo tails, sat beside her on the bench, and they played an impressive rendition of Chopsticks until both erupted with giggles.

Rachel pushed between them. "My turn."

His mom cleared her throat. "Maybe after supper. As much fun as it is listening to you guys. Food's getting cold. Come eat."

Later, after they'd eaten and cleared the dishes, Nick walked Sarah to her car while his mom helped Rachel with homework. The evening had been a taste of what their life together could be. What he dreamed about. He bit his tongue to keep from asking her right then and there to marry him so there could be nightly piano duets and trios.

Too soon. He was getting ahead of himself. She'd say no, for sure.

Plus, he needed to be sure Rachel loved Sarah as much as he did or none of his plan worked.

Stick to the plan. Stick to the plan. "We'll have to do this again."

"I'd love to. I'd forgotten how much I loved playing those old Guild pieces." She stood on tiptoe and brushed a kiss on his cheek. "Thank you."

The soft touch on his cheek broke him. His well-thought-out plan bit the dust. He took a deep breath and captured her face in his hands. "I'm going to kiss you because I can't help myself. Stop me if you don't feel the same."

He slowly lowered his lips to hers for a gentle, chaste kiss. Her lips were soft, velvety. He wanted more. So much more. He wanted forever. "Good night my sweet Sarah."

She made no reply, looking dumbfounded and as off-kilter as he felt. Questions ran across her face.

"It was just a good night kiss. And a really nice one at that."

"Nice." She echoed.

He opened her car door, and she slid inside. Stuffing his hands in his pockets, he stared until her rear car lights disappeared into the night. He could tell she'd felt something. That was good enough for now. Hope that had kicked him in the heart after he'd learned she'd never married took root.

He rubbed his cheek where she'd kissed him. Having her in his life wasn't just a plan. After tonight, it felt like a real possibility.

All he needed to do was figure out a way to tell her that Ethan was his new partner and would be coming back for Becca the way Nick had come back for Sarah.

Then everything would be golden... *IF* she accepted their plan and he could get Rachel on board. Everything hinged on those two things working out.

Chapter 6

Sarah hummed a happy tune all the way home. Her chin tingled from the feel of Nick's scratchy five o'clock shadow and the whisper of his mouth on hers. The prickling sensation shook loose every emotion she'd suppressed. Evenings like this with Nick and Rachel could be the life she'd always dreamed of.

Whoa, girl. That's a quantum leap. One kiss on the cheek, another butterfly kiss on the lips, and you're jumping to happily ever after. Look what happened when you did that at seventeen. One evening does not a fairy tale ending make. She gave her head a firm shake. *Stupid me.*

No time for romance anyway. All her energy needed to focus on convincing Rachel to agree to the surprise duet she hoped to pull off for the Christmas show's grand finale.

Busy. Yeah, that's what she told herself, but busy did nothing to quarantine her stuttering heart and family fantasies.

Or watching for Nick after his daughter's lessons.

At the end of Rachel's next lesson, Sarah brought up the duet idea. "Before you go, I have something to ask you. Would you do a Christmas duet with me at the end of the school Christmas program?"

Rachel's forehead wrinkled. "I've never played in front of strangers before."

"You'll do great. It'd give you practice playing in front of an audience before Guild competitions start next year."

"I don't know."

"We'll work together until it's perfect."

She tilted her head and did that little happy bounce of hers. "Okay. Sure. Dad will be so excited."

Sarah put her hand on the child's arm to still her. "Here's the thing. You can't tell him. Or anyone. It's a Christmas surprise. You'll have to practice when he and your granny are not listening, and we'll work on it together here."

"I can do that. Mom and I kept secrets all the time."

Sarah wondered what secrets but kept her mouth shut. "We're going to surprise everyone. Pinkie promise." She squeezed her pinkie around Rachel's.

"Now what are you two pinkie promising about?" Ms. Lorene appeared in the studio doorway.

Rachel gathered her music. "I can't say. It's a Christmas surprise." She winked at Sarah as she wiggled her pinkie.

"Right. See you next week." Sighing, Sarah waved her pinkie as they disappeared down the sidewalk. Once again, Nick hadn't come to pick his daughter up.

He kissed her and now suddenly he's avoiding her? It didn't make sense.

On Sunday, after their usual family lunch, Sarah and her sisters, pregnant sister-in-law, and future sister-in-law carried dishes from the table into the kitchen. They'd lost the coin toss used to determine who had to do cleanup, girls or boys. The guys, with smiley-face grins, followed her dad into the living room.

Andy's future wife, Darcy, walked beside her carrying a load of plates. "I hate washing all these by hand."

"I agree," Caleb's pregnant wife, Carrie, chimed in. "It's getting harder and harder for me to reach the sink." She patted her rounding belly.

"Cleanup isn't that bad when we all chip in." Her mom rinsed the last pan and handed it to Becca to dry.

"True enough, but one of these days you may not have to."

"Becca," Sarah hissed at her twin. They hadn't discussed their idea for all the siblings to pool resources to buy their folks a dishwasher for Christmas.

"Holiday secrets. It's getting to be that time, isn't it?" Faith grinned. "My most favorite time of the year."

Their mom smiled, dried her hands on her apron, and draped it over the oven handle. "Who's up for iced tea on the porch?"

With their glasses filled, the girls filed outside while the guys argued over an official call in the game they were watching. Pumpkins edged the porch steps alternating with pots of red and orange and gold chrysanthemums. Her mom's fall wreath of gourds entwined with colorful artificial fall leaves hung from the screen door. Sarah loved this time of year on the farm. An early cold front had blown in overnight and cooled temperatures down to the sixties. It actually felt like fall.

She settled into a rocking chair beside Darcy. "How are your wedding plans going? Spring will be here before we know it."

"Much better thanks to your mom stepping in to help. My momma's mobility issues were making it hard. Daddy tries, but what do men know about planning weddings?"

"Not much. Caleb thought his head was going to explode before we said, 'I do.' He just wanted all the fuss to be over." With a chuckle, Carrie eased her pregnant body into one of the other porch rockers.

"That's our Caleb. No nonsense. Straight to the

point. If he'd had his way, you two would have said you vows at the courthouse." Ms. Pat smiled at Darcy. "I'm happy to help. Groom-side of wedding stuff is not near as fun as the bride's. This way I get to work on both. Looks like my girls aren't going to be needing my help anytime soon anyway."

"Not me, for sure." Faith sat on the porch swing next to her mom.

Darcy grinned at Sarah. "With Nick Stephens back in town and available, that could change. Rumor has it, he and Sarah have been spending a lot of time together."

All eyes shifted to Sarah, who rubbed her toe into the space between planks on the porch floor, feeling every pigment of the strawberry circles heating her cheeks. "Nothing romantic. I helped him find a piano. That's all. His daughter's a gifted pianist, and Ms. Lorene's old piano doesn't hold a tune. They needed a new one."

Piano shopping, a dinner, and a breakfast plus brief visits if he picked up Rachel. Which he hadn't been doing lately. Almost seemed she'd dreamed that kiss like she had so many others through the years. She should stop with the pining for more, but she couldn't.

"You sure? You two *could* get back together." Carrie prodded.

"Rachel's been the only focus." Even Sarah could tell her voice had weakened. Her protest wasn't real. Having him back and ignoring her was killing her.

"But never fear, Mom. Sarah and I haven't given up on our twin wedding. One of these days, it'll happen. We're both still looking. Sarah, why don't you tell us what you have planned for your holiday program at school this year?" Her twin deftly changed the subject.

God bless Becca for rescuing her again.

"I've already started working with the kids on their grade level songs. We'll go into full rehearsal mode after Thanksgiving, which actually isn't that far off. And I'm working on another surprise finale."

With that the conversation drifted to holiday plans.

Sarah thanked Becca with a high five on the way out a short time later. "I owe you."

"TPS. You'd have done the same for me." Becca climbed into Sarah's car. "But, you know, you are gonna have to decide what to do about Nick Stephens. You two have been together a lot. Spontaneous dinner dates to talk about pianos, a family breakfast before piano shopping with lunch afterward, and another dinner with him at Ms. Lorene's to see the new piano. You can't tell me it's all been about Rachel."

"Well, no. He did kiss me when I went to see the new piano."

Becca gasped at the new detail.

"But zip since." Sarah cut her twin off before she could launch into questions. "He doesn't even come pick Rachel up from lessons. I'm not sure about this new Nick...he's different...changed."

"We've all changed. He's probably just been busy with work."

Sarah's shoulders slumped a little. "I guess. I'm confused about how to read him or separate my feelings for him from caring for his daughter."

"Sounds to me like you two need a proper date sans Rachel."

"I know, believe me, I know. But so far, she's always around. How am I supposed to start a conversation about his us?"

"Look, I'm not sure what to think about him either, but you obviously see something good. All I'm saying is be careful. Figure out what you want before you end up getting your heart broken again."

Sarah stared out the windshield. It might already be too late.

Chapter 7

The next Sunday, Sarah and Becca were on their way home after lunch when Sarah's phone chimed. "Will you see who that is?"

Becca peered at the caller ID. "Nick."

Sarah shook her head vigorously. "Let it go to voice mail."

"Hi, Nick. What's up? This is Becca."

Sarah sent her a fierce, mad face. Becca ignored her, pressed the speaker button. Nick's voice filled the small space.

"Hey, Becca. Y'all got away from church before I could talk to Sarah."

"You're on speaker. Sunday is family lunch. You forget?" Becca asked.

"Oh yeah. I did. But I do remember your mom's pot roast. Makes my mouth salivate thinking about it. She still making that?"

"Yep, with green beans and apple pie."

"Loved those apple pies and playing football in the yard."

"What did you want, Nick?" Sarah's voice sparked with a business tone.

A beat of silence followed her question before he said, "I was wondering if you two are up for an afternoon of board games? Mom's got something going with her Sunday School class here at the house. Rachel and I need some place to hang."

His voice sounded unsure. Was he nervous that he'd invited himself or worried she'd turn him down? Sarah rubbed the space between her eyebrows while the desire to say *sure* fought with the safety of saying *no*.

Waiting for Sarah to give her an answer, Becca hedged, "Hmm. Sounds like fun." Becca circled her hand in a hurry up movement.

"Thanks, Becca. Sarah, you up okay with us coming over?"

"Sure. It's fine. Give us thirty minutes."

"Thank you. We'll see you soon," Nick said above Rachel's background squeal of "Yes-s-s-s-s."

Sarah shot Becca a how-could-you scowl.

"Think about it. It's the perfect opportunity for you two to talk. I'll divert Rachel and give you time alone. Maybe you can find out what's going on." Grinning, her twin waved a thumbs up.

"Really? I'm not sure one afternoon will clear up a decade of hurt. One afternoon isn't going to provide a happily-ever-after or right everything with the man who destroyed my world."

"Whoa. Slow down. Relax. It's board games and hanging out. I'm not suggesting any of those things."

They drove in silence for a few minutes.

Sarah relaxed her grip on the steering wheel. "Sorry. I'm overreacting and I don't even know why."

Oh, but you do. You're terrified of risking your heart again.

"Come on, Sis. I know why. You're afraid to go down this road again. But you have to, so you'll know once and for all."

Spot on mindreading, again.

Only Sarah wasn't sure she still wanted a relationship with Nick. He'd left her behind. He was just as unpredictable now. Wasn't it safer to leave things as they were—being his daughter's teacher—rather than pretend Barb's ghost didn't loom between them?

No matter how much part of her heart wished it didn't matter, it did. She wasn't sure they could go back in time and make up for all they'd missed.

That first afternoon of games became a regular Sunday afternoon routine of playing board games together. Sometimes Ms. Lorene tagged along, or Sarah and Becca went to her house. But "the talk" never seemed to happen.

Absorbed in the games, competitive Becca forgot about her promise to slip away with Rachel.

Sarah didn't push. Status quo was safe. She found herself looking forward to the simple conversations and friendship she was rebuilding with Nick.

One Sunday Ms. Lorene didn't join them, and the snack stash ran dry. Even the hidden hoard of M&Ms disappeared.

"I can't keep losing to Rachel without M&Ms." Becca stood, executed a dramatic sigh, and dropped her head. "Y'all keep playing. I'll go pick up some."

"Can I go, Dad?"

Rachel's question must have triggered Becca's memory about their plan. She grabbed Rachel's hand. "Absolutely. Right, Nick?"

"Okay. But remember, Rachel needs to sit in the backseat. She hasn't quite grown enough to legally sit in the front seat yet."

"Gotcha." Becca pulled her keys from her purse. "We'll be back in a bit. You two keep playing." Her gaze locked with Sarah's. "Or talk."

Not so subtle, sister dear. Sarah readied the dominoes for another round of Mexican train. "Want to play?"

"Not really. I like Becca's idea. We need to talk. At least I do. I owe you an explanation." His gaze met hers. That now familiar-again feeling she was the only woman who mattered washed through her.

She squashed the thought. He had probably looked at Barb that same way. After all, he had traded their dreams for a life together for marriage with her.

"Talking won't change history." *Harsh, but his betrayal still stung.* Sarah stacked dominos into the tin and carried it to the closet.

"No. It won't. But I hope it'll help you understand. Maybe agree to give me a second chance." Nick tossed the throw pillows onto the floor, settled on the couch, and patted the cushion next to him. "Come sit by me."

Sarah didn't move. Her grip on the closet doorknob tightened while curiosity about how he'd explain breaking her teenage heart tugged her toward him.

"Please. I'm sorry I hurt you," he said in a small voice.

Sarah's heart thumped in her chest. Tangled emotions threatened to overwhelm her. When they were younger, she'd loved Nick with an intensity that had consumed her. Those feelings were a watered-down version of the emotions growing and soaring higher every day she was around this grownup Nick.

"Do you still love Barb?" The words popped out before she could stop them.

Nick's gaze held hers, steady. "I never loved Barb."

She sat with a heavy plop. "You *married* her." She wished she could take the condemning words back the second they left her mouth. But she couldn't. Wouldn't. All the nights filled with pain were in those words. She could hear it and knew he would.

"I was a schmuck."

Yes, yes you were. Except for parenting Rachel. She's a treasure. This time she didn't say the words aloud.

He wiped his hands along his thighs. "We'd had a bad argument about something. I don't even remember the specifics anymore, but you refused to talk to me. The guys on the team were going to a party like they usually did. My temper got the best of me and I went along. Frankly, I don't even remember the specifics of that fight anymore."

She didn't either. Most likely something blown out of proportion in her teenage insecure, hormone-plagued head. One minute wanting to be grownup, the next, hating the thought of going to a different college than Nick. Then—*bam*—he was marrying Barb and moving to Louisiana.

When she offered no response, he continued, his voice thin and weary. "Barb was there with her girlfriends. We were all drinking. I got drunk. But that's no excuse. I should never have gone to the party in the first place. Never taken that first beer. But I did. When she came on to me..." His shoulders rose and fell with a heavy sigh. "Two months later—after you and I'd gotten back together—she told me she was pregnant. The baby was mine. I believed her."

"So, you did the right thing. Very noble." Sarcasm warred with empathy in her words.

"Stupid. It ripped my heart in two that I'd betrayed you. After Rachel was born, Barb confessed she'd been with several others."

"But still you stayed." Sarah bit her tongue.

He stood, walked away. His expression was unreadable when he turned to face her again. "Once I held Rachel in my arms I couldn't leave. Didn't matter if she was mine or not."

Sarah pictured him cradling his newborn daughter, looking into that tiny face so innocent, so helpless. "I can understand that."

She didn't want to, but she did. How many times over the years had she imagined holding her own child, Nick's child, and watched friends with their babies wondering what it must be like?

He paced the living room from the bay window at the front to the French doors opening to the backyard. A hollow laugh escaped. "Being pregnant didn't work for with Barb. She wanted to keep on drinking and bar hopping with her friends."

Nick glanced over his shoulder at her. "To Barb's credit, after the doctor explained about Fetal Alcohol Syndrome, she stopped drinking. But up until then, she was the same party girl she'd always been. I worried, still worry, about the damage that might have been done before the doctor scared her straight."

"I'm a teacher. I know about FASD. I see none of the behavioral or learning problems in Rachel that I'd expect."

"And I thank God for that every day."

Nick walked back to the bay window, stuffed his hands in his pockets. He stood motionless for several long seconds before continuing, "I hired an *au pair* to help Barb after Rachel came home, but sadly, the call to party life was greater. Barb started drinking again and racked up DWIs." He faced Sarah again. "Before you ask, Rachel was never in the car with her."

"Why didn't you divorce her and sue for custody?"

"I did ask, thinking she'd welcomed the chance to be free, to relinquish the child who held her back. She said no. In her own way, Barb loved Rachel as much as I did. Joint custody was beyond scary. I couldn't risk it. I stayed for Rachel."

"Oh Nick, I'm sorry. You did the right thing but what a horrible life."

"I deserved to be miserable. Rachel didn't." He returned to the couch. "I took an office job. After enough DWIs, Barb joined AA. We agreed to work on the marriage for Rachel. Between counseling and parenting classes, we managed to forge a tentative truce, but love was never there."

A weighty silence curled between them as Nick waited for her response.

Sarah had none. She couldn't imagine living with someone she didn't love.

Chapter 8

The front door slammed open shattering the lengthening silence between Sarah and Nick. Rachel bounced in. "We're back."

Becca plopped three shopping bags on the table. Packages of candy tumbled out. "I may have gotten a little carried away."

"A little?" Sarah shook her head.

"We can't possibly eat all that. We'd—" Nick inflated his cheeks like a chipmunk. "Not to mention be sick as horses."

"It's not all for us, silly. I'll use most of it for the little stockings we give our students every year. The holidays are coming, you know." Becca gave Sarah a sly smile. "How'd you guys do?"

Silently, Sarah shot her sister the TPS code for "talk later." Aloud she said, "We just hung out here and visited."

She tried to make her voice sound normal. To be chill about all he'd told her like it was no big deal that he admitted he never loved Barb.

Not so easy. When deep inside, the NY philharmonic orchestra tuned up. He never loved Barb. Ever. He broke my heart to save Rachel's.

Rachel surveyed the kitchen table. "Hey, where's the game? I thought we were going to play some more."

"We were, but you still have homework to do before bedtime, and it's getting late." Nick tapped the end of her nose. "Maybe next Sunday you'll finish all your homework before we come."

"It's only a few problems. One more game, pretty please," Rachel whined.

Nick looked at his watch. "Well…"

Sarah moved next to him. "Your dad's right. Plus, I have lesson plans I haven't even started. We'll play again next Sunday."

Becca nodded. "Much as I'd like another chance to beat you. I agree. I still have a bunch of papers to grade. We'd better call it a night."

"But grownups can stay up as late as they want. I promise I only have five math problems. I'll have them done like that." She clicked her fingers in a snap.

"Rachel. Get your things. Now." His tone offered no other option.

If Rachel's eyes rolled any further back, she'd go blind. She stomped down the hallway like a Clydesdale.

Nick attempted to hide his smile, gave up. "Thanks, both of you, for backing me up. I was about to cave. She really loves these Sunday afternoons."

"We do too." Sarah looped her arm in his. "TPS can work for friends, you know."

"I'll keep that in mind." He leaned in, kissed her on the temple. "Thanks for listening. I hope you'll think about what I said. Give us a second chance."

The front screen door slammed. "Dad! Let's go." Rachel called on her way to his truck.

"I'm coming!" His hand circled Sarah's neck, catching her off guard. He kissed her squarely on the lips before jogging to his truck.

Her lips tingled from the pressure of his. A second chance with Nick. Wasn't that what she'd always hoped for?

"I saw that kiss," Becca called from the kitchen. "Come in here. I've made coffee." She set two mugs on the table. "All the deets. Spill."

"Basically, he said he'd never loved Barb. He only stayed for Rachel's sake." She recapped the details. "He wants a second chance."

Clapping her hands, Becca howled. "I knew it! So why do I hear hesitation in your voice?"

Sarah stared into her mug's black liquid as if it was one of those magic Eight Balls she'd played with as a kid, and an answer would appear. "Rachel. Nick's clearly devoted to her. She knows it. She has him wrapped around her little finger. That's a red flag. What if she doesn't want to share her dad?"

"Don't go there. You have a great relationship with Rachel. Ask her what she thinks of her dad dating."

"But what if—"

"Stop it. Rachel's not in charge of the world. His daughter's not Barb More important, Nick's not seventeen anymore. He'll deal with her. You saw how he handled her tonight. Now, I really do have papers to grade." Becca gave her a hug, grabbed her school tote, a handful of M&Ms, and disappeared into her bedroom.

Could it be that simple? Sarah wished.

Rachel came down the sidewalk alone for her next lesson. At the door, Sarah waved to her granny. *No Nick. Again.*

"She's not coming in?"

"Nah. She has to go to the store to get the baking stuff for the church's fall festival. I've never been to one of those. What's it like?"

"Loads of fun. Booths with games, crafts, and baked goods. Local artists come. Farmers bring their tractors to let kids have rides. Your granny's big turkey cookies are always a hit. You'll love it."

"That's what Granny says. She promised she'd save some cookies for me to decorate when I get home."

A memory pinged of sitting on a stool next to Nick in Ms. Lorene's kitchen putting sprinkles on cutout sugar cookies. Ms. Lorene always saved a cookie sheet full for them to finish after school. "I'm sure she will."

Sarah ushered Rachel inside. "Did you know

your dad and I used to help her decorate her cookies?"

"Granny said Dad did. You helped too?"

"I did. Your dad and I used to do lots of things together."

"Granny told me you were friends when you were in school."

"She did?" Sarah searched for any sign of disapproval. Rachel nodded, but her expression remained neutral.

Here's your opening. Sarah hesitated but decided not to press the issue. Instead, setting up the duet sheet music on the piano. "Let's go over our song before Becca shows up."

They ran through their duet several times working on rough spots. Hers, not Rachel's. "It's sounding great. We'll need to start memorizing soon."

"Dad is going to be so happy. He talks all the time about what fun it is listening to us play."

"It is, isn't it?" Sarah took a deep swallow. *Another chance. Bite the bullet. Ask her. It's the perfect opportunity.* "What would you think if your Dad and I became friends again like we used to be?"

Sarah held her breath as she exchanged the duet music with Rachel's lesson book, one eye watching for Rachel's reaction.

Rachel squiggled on the piano bench, swung her feet. "He doesn't have many friends. Granny and I are all he's got. She's his mom. Moms are your friend no matter what. He could really use a grownup friend. He didn't have any girl kind of friends at all where we lived before, you know."

Sarah's heart hit a high C. *Interesting.* "I'd love to be your dad's friend. And yours. Not just your teacher."

Gee, I sound like Mr. Rogers.

Rachel dipped her head. "I'd like that."

Sarah flipped the lesson book open, nonchalantly pressed her finger down the middle seam to hold it open. "Now, how 'bout we focus on the piece you've been working on."

After the lesson, Sarah glanced out the studio window hoping to spot Nick's truck. No such luck. Ms. Lorene's big tank of a sedan waited at the curb.

Chapter 9

Early Saturday morning, Sarah meandered through the church bazaar booths watching vendors complete setup. Becca preferred to sleep in, but Sarah had wanted to check out the selections before the crowds arrived. Suddenly, hands clamped around her waist, squeezed. "Boo!"

She turned to see Nick.

"I figured I'd find you here. You always liked to check out the choices in the booths early."

"And, unlike my lazy twin, you always came with me. Where's Rachel?"

"Helping Mom." He clasped her hand and pulled her behind the big oak tree in the field. "Rachel told me about your conversation." He lifted her chin until their eyes met. "I hear you'll be my *girl*friend."

"I'm not sure Rachel meant girlfriend the way you're saying. Or that we can just pick up where we left off."

He cupped her face. "I agree. But friendship is a great place to start, don't you think?"

His lips were inches from hers. Sarah willed her heels to cement themselves to the ground, so she didn't close the distance. The cement didn't hold. Her heels lifted—

"Dad!" Rachel charged toward them holding hands with a friend.

Sarah and Nick jumped apart as fast as they had the time Deacon Wilson caught them behind the same tree.

Nick muttered, "My kid has the worst timing."

"Oh, hi, Miss Sarah." Rachel's smile morphed to a frown, which Sarah interpreted as disapproval. "My friend Catherine says there's going to be a hayride tonight. Can we go, Dad, please?"

"Sure. Sarah and I used to go on the fall festival hayride every year." He turned to Sarah. "What do you say? You want to join us?"

Chestnut brown eyes filled with hope held hers. Those hayrides had been magical. Romantic. Becca and Ethan, her and Nick. The big harvest moon overhead. "I'd love to," she answered.

"But I meant us." Rachel circled with her finger between Catherine, Nick, and herself.

Nick ignored his daughter's comment. "Now Sarah will join us."

"But Dad…"

"It's settled, Rachel. Sarah, we'll pick you up at seven."

Sarah stepped back. Confusion had her hesitating. Her instincts had been right. Rachel said she wanted Sarah to be Nick's friend, but clearly, she didn't want her along on the hayride. Not a good start.

"I can go with Becca. See you at the bonfire."

"No. It's a date. You're coming with us."

A date? Did it even count as a date if the daughter who didn't want her there was along?

She wasn't sure. It'd been a long time since she'd dated. Never with a widower who had a daughter. Never with the man she'd loved for a bajillion years even after he broke her heart.

New territory. Strange territory. Hard-to-navigate territory. She had a lot to learn.

Seven o'clock sharp, Nick pulled his pickup to the curb at Sarah's. Wearing fresh-pressed jeans from the cleaners and a plaid shirt Rachel picked out, he felt like a goofball teenager on his first date.

Becca opened the door. "Sarah's grabbing a jacket. She'll be right here."

Nick was about to give a flippant response when Sarah strolled out. Hair in a messy bun. Rosy blush to her cheeks. Bone-melting smile. The exact same smile that used to bring him to his knees. It hadn't lost its power.

"Ready?" he squeaked.

"Ready."

Becca waved from the doorway. "See y'all there."

Nick opened the truck door and held Sarah's hand as she lifted her foot to the running board and pole-vaulted herself into the seat. She smiled her thanks.

"Where's Rachel?" she asked when he climbed in the driver's side.

"Catherine's mom offered to drive the girls." He'd wanted to shout "Thank you, Lord" into the phone. He needed a break from his daughter, and his daughter needed to accept that he was going to spend time alone with Sarah.

"That's great. Friends will help her settle in better."

"True. She's been a bit clingy since we moved in with Mom. Well, since she lost Barb. I think she's afraid she's going to lose me too."

"Losing her mom the way she did, it's understandable."

"I try to be patient." He reached over and took Sarah's hand. "But I'm ready to have my own life back." Someday Rachel would leave to start her new life. Being alone was never his plan. Having Sarah back was.

The autumn sun was beginning its descent when they walked toward the wagons a short drive later. Rachel came running over. "Catherine and I aren't read to ride yet. It okay if we wait for the next wagon?"

Nick glanced at Sarah. She smiled. "Sure," he said and sent a thank you prayer heavenward.

Sarah braced her hand on his shoulder to step up into the wagon then moved to the front of the trailer behind the tractor. The place they'd always selected so her dad, or whoever was driving, couldn't see them easily.

When you dated the preacher's kid people always watched. Guess that never changed. He was with her again. That was all that mattered. He'd deal with watchful eyes because this time he wasn't blowing it.

He grinned, loving the night already.

Sarah scooted closer to him as another couple loaded on and squeezed next to them. With all the spaces filled, the wagon jerked forward. At the jolt, Nick slipped his arms around Sarah to steady her. She resisted at first, but he didn't let go. Her head relaxed against his shoulder as the tractor bounced over the uneven field.

Her younger brother Sammy waved his guitar in the air. "Taking requests. Let's play who can stump Sarah."

"Not possible. Sarah knows them all," the driver called out. "How about we start with "Father Abraham," one of my favorites."

Recognizing Pastor Fitz's voice, Nick swallowed a groan. Sarah's dad driving. Sammy on guitar. All eyes were on him and Sarah. This *was* just like old times.

When the wagon circled back to the start, Nick jumped to the ground, took Sarah by the waist, and lifted her down. Her eyes sparkled in the moonlight. "That was such fun. I haven't been on a hayride since..." she squeezed her eyes shut. Her voice wobbled. "...in a long time."

His heart tightened in his chest. They both knew she meant since he'd disappeared with Barb. He released a jagged breath. He couldn't undo the past or rewrite it, but somehow he'd make up for the years they'd lost.

Chapter 10

After the hayride, Sarah noticed changes in their relationship. Nick called her just to talk. Not daily, but frequently. He picked Rachel up from lessons more. When he did, he took them for dinner, or brought something to share after the lessons. They never missed Sunday afternoon games.

And Rachel seemed to be okay with Sarah being along.

All should have been good.

But it wasn't. Sarah couldn't pinpoint why or shake the uneasy feeling Nick was avoiding commitment. They never spoke of the growing connection and, except for the hayride, Rachel was always with them. Well, not on the phone calls, but in person.

Why didn't he ever want to be with her, alone? Rachel was always with them.

Becca cornered her after they left Ms. Lorene's one Sunday. "Your forehead looks like a corn field after the dead stalks have been ploughed. Why the worry lines? Did something happen between you and Nick?"

"No. That's the problem." How did she say this without sounding overly childish? "We're never alone. I love being with Rachel, but we need some time for ourselves, you know."

Becca nodded with a wistful, faraway look in her eyes. "I do. As much fun as our double dates used to be, Ethan and I always wanted time to ourselves."

"Exactly. Don't you think if Nick were truly interested, he'd ask me on a date by now? He hasn't."

"Dating is tricky for a single dad."

Sarah gave an exaggerated eyeroll. "Not that tricky! He lives with his mother."

"Maybe he's playing it safe and waiting for you to make the next move. Giving you space to back out or go as slow as you need. Girls ask guys out these days. Ask him yourself." Becca huffed. "Don't let the chance to be with your one true love slip away. You can't tell me Nick isn't your one true love."

"Same as Ethan is yours."

Her sister's face went to stone.

Sarah regretted the sarcastic quip the moment she threw those words out. "Sorry. I shouldn't rehash all that."

It wasn't Becca's fault Ethan had disappeared off the face of the planet. At least Sarah had known why Nick abandoned her. That didn't make her pain any less real, though.

"Apology accepted. But I've watched you pine

away all these years for what you two lost. You're back together. You have another chance. What's stopping you?"

Sarah see-sawed her shoulders to break up the knots of tension building in her neck. "I have not been pining."

Lying to yourself again. Geez.

Becca narrowed her eyes. Not buying it either.

"Okay. That's a lie, but what if we don't belong together anymore?"

"Anyone that sees you together knows that's not true. He needs a little nudge. Ask him out."

Sarah pushed off the couch. "Don't you have papers to grade or something?"

The week before Thanksgiving, her mom called. "I wanted you to know I've invited Lorene and her family for the holiday."

Sounded like something Becca orchestrated. Her twin had been bugging her about asking Nick for a date ever since their talk. Queen of procrastination, Sarah never found the right moment. "Becca put you up to that?"

"Maybe. But I think it's a great idea. Rachel will have a chance to meet the whole family."

"But there won't be anyone there her age."

"Not true. Andy's bringing one of his students like he always does. Remember, Martin Cortez, the one raising his little sister? She's coming with him, and she's Rachel's age."

Give it up, girl. Mom will have an answer for every objection. Sarah groaned. "Fine."

Becca had the whole family plotting. She never should have mentioned her doubts. Her twin's romantic soul wouldn't quit until Sarah and Nick walked down the aisle.

Thanksgiving Day went well. Wonderful. Sitting on the porch watching the two girls on the oak tree swing and Nick play football with her brothers, Sarah felt like being a family was a real possibility, until…

The football game broke up. The guys joined the gals on the porch. Nick squeezed onto the porch swing between her and Becca. He slid his arm across Sarah's shoulders and tucked her close to whisper, "I want us to have dozens of Thanksgiving days as a family like this."

Sarah nuzzled closer. That had always been her dream.

Then Andy's student Matt announced he and his sister were leaving.

After which Ms. Lorene said, "Rachel, why don't we head home? We can work on our fruit cake baking."

"Let's go, Dad." Rachel smiled at Nick.

"I thought I'd hang here with Sarah and the others for a little while longer." He gave Sarah's shoulder a squeeze. The way his eyes darted to her mouth left no doubt about what was really on his mind.

Rachel's face turned red. "But you *have* to come. You do the chopping when Granny gets tired. She won't let me use the knife."

Nick stiffened. "You go along with Granny. I won't be late. I can still help."

"You're old enough now. I'll show you how." Ms. Lorene sent Nick a hopeful look.

Rachel planted her feet. "No. If Dad's gonna stay, I'm not leaving."

Ms. Lorene sucked in a breath. "Young lady, if your Dad wants to stay, he certainly can." She reached for Rachel's hand. "You come along with me."

Rachel jerked her hand from Ms. Lorene's. "I want to stay with Dad."

Nick's eyes shifted as if he were comparing notes on a mental blackboard. It was clear he didn't want to give in. But, because he thought he should really leave or because he didn't want a showdown in front of her family, either way their day together was over.

Sighing, he slapped his palms on his knees, shoved up from the swing. "Sounds like I need to do some chopping." He turned to her parents. "Thank you for the lovely day." His eyes met hers. "I'll call you later."

He held the stair railing in a relaxed grip, but Sarah could tell he was anything but.

Her brothers and Dad disappeared inside to

watch yet another football game. Darcy headed to the front door. "Y'all come help me pick out bridesmaid dresses. I brought magazines."

"A bride who lets the bridesmaids pick out the dresses. I'm in." Faith followed Darcy.

Carrie hefted herself from the porch rocker. "Think there are any maternity choices?"

The porch swing creaked as Becca shifted and cast a questioning glance Sarah's way.

"Go on." Her mom shooed Becca off and settled into the spot Nick had vacated. She patted Sarah's thigh. "We'll be along in a bit."

After the others had gone inside, her mom toed the swing gently. "I don't envy Nick's position. He's carrying a heavy load."

"I know, Mom. So's Rachel. She watched her mom die for goodness sake. That's a horrible thing to deal with. I think it's why she clings to Nick so tightly." She pursed her lips debating whether to go on. She felt so selfish. Teenage-girl selfish. But her mom had always been her best listener. "It's just if Nick and I hope to have a relationship we have to have time together. He's guilt parenting. I understand. I'm just not sure *we* can survive. *Will* survive."

Her mom took her hand, held it to her heart. "You will. You two belong together. Give him some time."

Sarah felt an unpleasant chill at the back of her neck, blinked several times, and swallowed. "I hope you're right, but it may be too late for us."

Chapter 11

"Everything okay over there?" Sarah asked when Nick finally called after Rachel's bedtime.

"If you mean with the chopping, no one got hurt. Rachel now knows how to rock the big chef's knife holding the point instead of guillotining whatever she's cutting up. Mom has enough nuts to last till Christmas and beyond."

Sarah laughed.

"I hated leaving like that, but Rachel wasn't giving up, and I didn't want one of her Barb scenes."

"What do you mean *Barb* scene?"

"Rachel grew up watching her alcoholic mother throw fits to get her way. Rachel's been practicing the technique. Not a pretty sight. Dr. Mara says she's reacting to all the changes in her world."

So far, Rachel's displays of disobedience felt directed toward their relationship. At least to Sarah. There'd been no rebellion, no scenes at school.

"It must seem like I cave to her every time. I don't. Mara says to pick my battles. Today didn't seem like the battle."

She'd give him that. "Probably not. But it wasn't the first time she's made you choose between me and her. She has to be on board with an us if *we're* going to have any kind of a relationship."

That was Sarah's biggest worry. She and Rachel needed to share his heart. Not force him to choose one over the other.

"Maybe we need to back off. Give Rachel more time to accept us. More sessions with her therapy." *Not what I truly want, but what was best.*

"I have a plan."

She gave a soft laugh. "Right. You always had a plan."

"I did and I do. This one's a great plan."

"A great plan, huh? Better than the one you came up with when Dad caught us in the choir loft?" She'd been grounded for a month after that one. If this new plan was anything like that, they'd never get their happily ever after.

He chuckled. "Lots better. Don't give up on me."

That was what her mom had said. Sarah hoped they were both right. Sneaking rendezvous behind Rachel's back wasn't a good plan. The child needed to accept them as a couple if they ever hoped to be a family.

Sunday afternoon after Thanksgiving when Nick and Rachel arrived for games, he sent Becca a conspiratorial wink.

Uh-oh! This can't be good. Sarah went on full alert.

"I thought maybe instead of playing games today we could head to the Christmas tree farm. That sound like a good idea?" Nick asked.

"Yeah!" Rachel gave him a high five.

Becca grabbed the domino game tin from Sarah. "Excellent idea."

"But we have the artificial one in the attic. You could help us get it down," Sarah said.

Nick shook his head. "With a Christmas tree farm practically in your backyard, I can't believe you use a fake tree."

Sarah tugged the game from Becca. "Because holidays are crazy times for teachers. All our energy goes to corralling students hyped up about Santa, not tracking down the perfect tree. It's quicker to just pop a fake one out of the box and voilà, a tree that works. We're hardly here over the holidays, anyway. We spend Christmas Eve and Christmas Day at Mom and Dad's."

Sarah was fighting a losing battle. Her romantic twin was charging full speed ahead. Family Thanksgiving together. Now Christmas tree shopping. The Hallmark moments were piling up.

Or was this part of Nick's plan?

He jingled his keys and pulled Sarah's coat from the rack by the door. "Not this year."

Becca shooed them all out the door.

Another Hallmark movie scene, here we come.

The tree was up, all the new lights glowing. The fragrance of the fresh cut tree saturated the room. They stood back admiring it.

"Thanks for all the manual labor, Nick. Now you understand why we go the artificial route."

Nick moved behind Sarah, dropped his arms over her shoulders, and pulled her against his very firm chest. His chin rested on her head. His heart beat against her spine. She never wanted the moment to end.

"I do and you're welcome."

Awe glistened in Rachel's eyes. "It's gonna be wonderful with the decorations on it. Can we get a live one for Granny's house?"

"Perhaps. We'll ask her. Decorating will have to wait for another day, though. It took longer than I thought to find a tree. We need to head home. It's late."

"But Dad," Rachel pleaded.

"It's a school night."

"That's so not fair. I want to decorate. It's the fun part."

"Maybe your dad will let you stay over after lessons tomorrow. You can help us then." Becca turned to Sarah. "That okay with you?"

"Pretty please, Miss Sarah," Becca and Rachel said in unison, ganging up on her once again.

"Sure. If your Dad agrees. You're my last student of the day."

Rachel pulled her fists in a *yes* gesture. "Thank you, thank you."

"At least give me a chance to say yes." Nick laughed. "Now get your things together. We'll be on our way."

Rachel headed toward an ornament box. "How about I hang just one first?"

"Rachel." The warning in his voice was clear. She disappeared into the music room for her backpack and music satchel.

Nick faced Sarah. "It's been a perfect afternoon. If we were alone right now, I'd..."

He pressed closer. Sarah was sure he was going to kiss her. She closed her eyes. His lips had barely brushed hers when, as if on cue, Rachel called. "Are we going or what?"

"Be right there." He bent forward for what Sarah hoped was a proper goodbye kiss.

Rachel stomped into the room. "You said we—" Her eyes widened at seeing Sarah in Nicks arms. "Dad, you said we needed to go."

"Yeah. Ok." Sneaking a kiss to Sarah's temple so quick nobody would notice, he dropped his arms, leaving a chill in the air. "We'll see you tomorrow. I'll bring dinner."

He executed a one-eighty and disappeared out the door, his back stiff.

Oh, to be a fly on the dashboard for that ride home. That was the closest he'd come to being affectionate in front of Rachel. Maybe Sarah did need to be patient like her mom said. With a smile, she headed to the kitchen. "I'm getting more hot chocolate. Want some?"

"Sounds wonderful."

Sarah carried two mugs to the living room and plopped onto the couch to stare at the seven-foot Douglas Fir Christmas tree with a star on top, standing magnificent in the bay window. The small white lights twinkled like snowflakes in moonlight. Even with no ornaments, she loved the tree they'd picked out. Like a family would do. "Nick was right. A live tree is better."

"The evergreen smell is wonderful." Becca inhaled deeply. "I can't wait to see the ornaments on it. Rachel sure wanted to do them tonight. So did I."

"She did." Sarah mustered her best frown. "But I wish you hadn't suggested she stay after her lesson tomorrow."

"Why not? From the looks you two shared all day, I'd think you'd welcome more time together." Becca fanned herself.

"Yeah. Rachel picked up the vibes. The day had been wonderful until that nearly kiss. She didn't seem very pleased."

"That was just a kid's reaction to parental PDA. Nick will handle it."

"I hope you're right. I just don't have a good feeling."

Sarah awoke the next morning with her heart racing after a night of what-could-be dreams. The old teenage flush was as strong as it had ever been. Stronger.

Was she being delusional? Since Nick had returned, she'd been on such a roller coaster. One day high and hopeful, the next sinking sand.

He hadn't said he loved her. Only that he'd never loved Barb and someday hoped to have a new mommy for his daughter. Just because he didn't love Barb didn't mean he loved Sarah or wanted her to be Rachel's new mom.

Especially if Rachel objected. Nick adored his daughter. He carried a ton of guilt about how he'd allowed Barb to treat her, what the child had been through.

Sarah wasn't sure she'd win that contest.

Chapter 12

Nick collected his thoughts as he walked to the truck with Rachel. The cold air stung like the tension between them.

He opened the truck's back door. She tossed in her stuff, slid under his arm, and hefted herself inside. Nick jogged to the driver's side. When he heard the click of his daughter's seatbelt, he turned the key in the ignition. The truck roared to life.

He dialed the heater to full blast. "You warming up back there?" He watched her in the rear mirror.

"No." Her tone carried the tween impertinence that had begun to explode a lot lately.

He resisted the urge to call her on it, remembering the therapist's caution to pick his battles. "Something we need to talk about?"

No response.

"Sarah, maybe?"

He glanced in the mirror again. Her lips pursed. Her hands shoved under her armpits. More mad than cold now.

"I thought you wanted Sarah and me to be friends. We're friends."

She gave an acknowledging nod. Her lips relaxed ever so slightly. The frown remained.

"What's the problem? You like doing things with her. How she's teaching you to play the piano. Don't you?"

Her forehead furrows relaxed. A little.

He unclenched the steering wheel. Blood circulated to his bare knuckles. "And picking out the tree was fun."

She shrugged. "Yeah. It was."

"And you're going to help her decorate tomorrow. More fun." He checked the mirror. "So, what don't you like about me being her friend?"

"Friends don't kiss each other on the lips."

Bingo! His gut had been right. Jealous just like her mother. "Sometimes they do if they really like each other."

"Mom said they don't."

Nick cringed. Rachel had heard his arguments with Barb. No telling what else Barb had fed her when he wasn't around. "But if a single guy really likes a woman, kissing happens."

"No, only moms and dads kiss like that."

"They do, but when you really like someone and she's your very good friend you kiss them." *Present the idea slowly. Let Rachel get used to it. Mara, I pray you're right.* "And, if you really, really like a girl, you can become a family." He held his breath.

"You like Sarah like that?" Rachel's voice wobbled.

"I do. Is that okay with you?"

Her frown lines were back. "I guess so."

"Then if I kiss Sarah, it's not gonna be a problem with you." Nick pulled into the driveway of his mom's house and shifted to look at her.

She unbuckled, gathered her stuff, and lifted her head. "I guess not."

Her tone was less than convincing. But, for now, he'd count the positive response as progress. They'd discuss the other part of his plan, the part about having Sarah join their family, another time.

His boots hit the ground with a thud. He rounded the truck to open her door. "Go get your bath. I'll come read to you when you're ready," he said when they were inside.

"I want a bubble bath." The tween tone was back.

"Fine, but don't dawdle. You have twenty minutes."

"Forty minutes. It takes time to fill the tub."

"Twenty. You're wasting time arguing. Go."

She stomped down the hallway.

His mom muted the TV. "Uh oh. Trouble?"

Nodding, Nick rolled his shoulders. "I need something to drink."

"Sweet tea or Dr. Pepper." His mom started to stand.

Nick motioned her to stay. "I can get it."

His mom's limited beverage options always

bugged the Barb even during her sober times. Why had that popped into his head? *Because you're afraid your daughter's becoming a Barb.*

Dr. Pepper can in hand, he returned to the living room and sank into his dad's old recliner. His mom turned the TV off. "What's wrong?"

"Rachel's acting jealous towards Sarah. Like Barb used to do any time I so much as looked at another woman."

He wasn't going to get specific about how he'd been kissing Sarah. Not with his mom, even if he was a grown man. *TMI.*

His mom bit her lip. Concerned laced her words. She'd witnessed many of Barb's jealous rages in person. "What do you mean?"

"She demands my attention if I'm anywhere near Sarah." He popped the tab on his soda. "And it's escalating."

"I don't think that's so unusual. She's lost her mom. She doesn't want to share her dad."

"But she won't. I tell her all the time she's my number one girl. I include her in everything I do with Sarah so she can see how good things could be as a family. I never could convince Barb. I'm not doing any better with Rachel. She's heard most of Barb's nasty arguments where she accused me of not loving her and screaming all I wanted was to go back to Miss PKPP."

His mom's hand flew across her mouth and chin. "Oh, my. I'm not sure I want to know what Miss PKPP stands for?"

"Miss Preacher Kid Pretty Princess. Rachel has no idea that's Sarah."

"That's awful."

"Barb could be especially hateful when she was drunk." Nick gave a heavy sigh. "It's made Rachel as insecure as Barb was. I'm worried. What if I can't convince Rachel?"

"I think the bigger worry is what if she figures out your past connection with Sarah? We all promised we wouldn't tell her about your history, but you just never know."

"I understand, and I will tell her the whole story someday. But for now, Rachel just needs to see how great Sarah is."

"The older she gets the better she'll understand."

"But at her age, she doesn't. That's why I'm waiting to mention our past boyfriend/girlfriend-gonna-get-married-someday relationship."

Sarah had gone along with that quiet, even agreed to convince Becca and her family to keep their secret. Although, he was fairly sure her consent was based more on uncertainty about whether she wanted to renew that relationship than if they would.

"You'll know when the time's right."

"Delaying's risky, but Ethan convinced me you have to take risks to get what you want, especially when what you want is worth it. Sarah definitely is."

His mom shrugged. "You're right. You and Sarah belong together, but, if Rachel's already acting jealous, you might regret not telling her."

"Exactly." He rubbed his neck. "But I'm ready to move on with my life. That's a life with Sarah. I have to take the risk."

"I understand, sweetheart. That's why I tried to get Rachel to come home with me on Thanksgiving so you two could have time together."

He took a swig from the can. "I appreciated that. When Rachel balked, I left because I didn't want to risk a Barb scene in front of everyone."

"Rachel does like Sarah, she's told me."

Nick grinned. "True. She's told me the same thing, but her attitude lately makes me feel like I'm back in high school having to choose. I don't want to hurt Rachel, but I can't lose Sarah again."

"Dad." Rachel called from her bedroom.

Nick pushed out of the recliner. "Wish me luck. I'm going to tell her I'm inviting Sarah to my office Christmas party."

His mom grabbed his hand as he passed and kissed his fingers. "I'm praying. Have faith. This *will* work out."

He leaned forward and gave her a hug. "Love you."

After tucking Rachel in, Nick came back down-stairs.

"Well?" his mom asked.

"No objections after reassurances that Sarah wasn't ever going to replace her. Now I have to hope Sarah will say yes." He held up crossed fingers.

She smiled. "That's a given."

"I hope so. A lot's riding on her being with me at the party."

Chapter 13

Rachel was already adding ornaments to the tree when Nick arrived after her lesson the next day. He kissed his daughter's head with a nod toward the Christmas tree. "Looking good. Looking very good. Think you can stop long enough to eat a hot dog? I stopped at Dairy Shack."

"I love their dogs." Rachel raced ahead to the kitchen table. "Come on, Miss Becca."

Nick wiggled the sack toward the twins. "Hope you still like strawberry shakes and corny dogs. There's chocolate for yours, Becca."

Sarah's face lit with approval. "I can't believe you remembered."

He winked. "I remember a lot."

Rachel ate her hot dog in about three bites. Determined to get every last drop, she sucked down her shake until a freight train whistle squeaked in their ears. "Gotta go. There's still a lot of ornaments." She dashed back to the living room.

Becca followed close behind. "You two finish. I'll supervise."

Once they were out of sight, Nick whirled Sarah into his arms, squeezed her tight before he lowered his mouth gently to hers. "I've thought about that all day long. Been hard to concentrate."

Sarah gave him a half-hearted push. "Rachel could pop back in here any second."

"Sneaking kisses again, isn't it great?"

"No, it isn't. Didn't you notice your daughter's reaction last night? I don't think she's ready for her dad to be kissing me or anyone else."

"Sarah, Sarah." He kissed the tip of her nose. "Of course, I did. We talked on the way back to Mom's. She's fine with kissing. With us kissing."

And to prove his point, he tugged her tightly to his chest, bent his head, and kissed her again. Gently at first, then his lips firmed over hers. He never wanted to let go.

Sarah's senses reeled as if short-circuited. All doubts from the night before exploded into sparks with the warm pressure of his lips. Rachel was fine with them. But he still hadn't asked her on a date. *What was up with that?*

It's the twenty-first century, you should ask him. Becca was right.

Sarah planted her feet before her courage dissolved. "Nick, I..."

"Sarah, I've..." he said, at the same time, shifting weight from foot to foot in a familiar nervous action. Uncertainty slithered up her spine again.

"You go first." Sarah clamped her back teeth waiting for another Barb bombshell.

"There's something... I've been wanting...to I should have..." He stilled, met her gaze squarely. "Will you go with me to my company Christmas party?"

Relief swished through her body. She stood on tiptoes and kissed him softly. "I'd love to, Nick Stephens."

"Dad," Rachel's voice called from the living room. "We can't reach to hang ornaments high. Come help."

"That kid of mine has the gift for interrupting at the most inopportune times. On our way, Rachel." Nick slid his arm around Sarah's shoulder, cupping her into his side. "We'll talk details later."

Rachel greeted them swinging a hand-painted wooden ornament. "I just love this Santa. Did you paint it, Miss Sarah?"

"One of my students did. I hang all the home-made ornaments I get. That's one of my favorites."

"Some are mine." Becca pulled another one out of the box and held up a felt teddy bear decorated with sequins. "Like this one."

Sarah lifted a counted cross-stitch piano in a small embroidery hoop. "This one's mine for sure."

"Your own baby grand, finally." Nick gave Sarah a high five.

Scowling, Rachel crooked her finger, calling Nick over. "Help me put Santa up high where he can be seen. Like there." She pointed to a spot out of her reach. He lifted her.

"Guess what?" he said as he lowered her to the floor. "Miss Sarah said yes to my office party." He beamed.

Becca waved a thumps-up. "I knew she would."

"You asked Becca first?"

"Had to be sure TPS wasn't going to squelch my move."

Sarah's shoulders shook as the giggle gurgled up like a geyser. "TPS really worries you, doesn't it?"

"You have no idea," he answered.

Rachel shot Sarah an evil eye. "He asked me if I was okay with it, too."

Sarah flinched at her tone and the implication. Would Nick have asked her if his daughter had said no? The uncertainty stole some of her joy. Would a relationship with Nick always mean a competition with his daughter? She dug out a pageant smile. "Well thank you for saying yes."

"What's this one?" Rachel held up a brass ornament cradle.

"Dad gave Mom two the year we were born. She passed them on to us for our Christmas tree when we moved out," Becca answered. "Check the engraving. The name will tell you whether it's mine or Sarah's."

Nick peered into the box with his daughter. "I remember when we all bought ones like this at the mall kiosk." His gaze grabbed Sarah's and held.

For a moment, she was lost in a fog of Christmas past. The hopeful promise of Christmases future.

"What's this one?" Rachel held up a kissing couple.

Sarah's eyes shifted from Nick to Becca. Rachel didn't know she and Nick had been more than just friends before. A Christmas ornament felt like a terrible way to spring the truth on her, regardless of how "okay" she was with them kissing.

Becca, being closer, reached for the ornament.

Rachel held tight, flipping it around to read the engraving. "It says Becca and Ethan."

A collective sigh of relief echoed in the room.

"Ethan was my boyfriend in high school. We both got them from our boyfriends. I'll take it." Becca gave a phony laugh. "Don't know why I kept it."

Not exactly true. Becca knew why, same as Sarah did. Ethan and Nick had been their only boyfriends. Neither of them could bear not hanging the ornament memory each year.

"Really? So...there's one in here for Sarah and her boyfriend?" With a twinkle in her eye, Rachel turned her full attention to shifting through the assortment of brass ornaments.

Sarah's heart pounded like a kettle drum.

Nick stuffed his hands in his pockets, as much at a loss as to how to get out of this as Sarah was.

TPS to the rescue.

Becca snatched the box. "Let's save the rest to put on the tree later."

"Great idea," Sarah's voice sounded like she had an oboe reed lodged in her throat.

Rachel yanked the box from Becca, ignoring them both, and continued to fish around, finally lifting out a second couple kissing. "Here it is."

Her eyes widened as she read, "Nick and Sarah." She whipped around to face her dad. "You were Sarah's boyfriend?"

Another lie about it not being the same Nick flittered through Sarah's head. She dismissed it immediately. After their big omission, another lie would only come back to bite them harder. Her eyes pleaded with Nick to respond.

He squatted. "That was a long, long time ago, sweetheart. Before your mom and I."

Rachel pointed at the ornament. "But it says the year I was born." Innocent eyes, rimmed with confusion, went from one to the other. "Sarah's Miss PKPP? The one Mom meant?" Each word slowly and distinctly enunciated climbed an octave higher.

The Christmas clock chimed eight-thirty. The twangy notes of "It Came Upon a Midnight Clear" coated the room in silence as bright as the star had illuminated the holy night.

The song ended. Several beats ticked by until Rachel's voice cracked the silence. "She's why we came back here to live, isn't she? So you can be with Miss PKPP just like Mom always said you would."

Nick passed the ornament to Sarah then took

Rachel's shoulders in his hand, looked her in the eyes. "No, it's not like that."

Rachel jerked away. "Mom was right. You never loved us. I want to go home." Sarah squeezed the ornament in her hand until the sharp edges dug into her skin as Rachel ran out the door to the truck.

Nick rose slowly. "I'll call later." His eyes didn't leave Sarah's, but they weren't as bright as they had been moments before. His steps heavier, as if the yoke tethering him to the life he'd made for himself, weighed him down.

Sarah wanted to reassure him, to say they could get through this, but in her heart of hearts, she wasn't sure. Rachel would never be ok with him kissing her now, let alone creating a family together.

As the door closed, Becca gave her a hug. "Nick will explain to her. It'll work out."

Sarah dropped her head on her sister's shoulder, fought to hold back the gathering tears. "After everything Barb's imprinted in Rachel's heart. How can he...how can I ever undo that kind of anger and hurt?"

This was the end of her and Nick.

Probably forever this time.

Chapter 14

After first period the next day, Becca found Sarah. "Thought you'd want to know Rachel's not in school."

"It's got to be because of what happened last night."

Becca lifted her shoulders in a shrug. "What did Nick say when he called?"

"We haven't talked." She couldn't figure out why he hadn't called. Surely, he knew she'd be on pins and needles worried about running into Rachel in the hallway. Until he told her what had happened with his daughter, she would have to peek around corners to avoid her.

"But it doesn't make sense. She seemed so happy when you agreed to go to his office party."

"I know," Sarah sighed. "We should have told her about our past relationship."

The tardy bell rang. "Perhaps. I don't think it would have made a difference." Becca gave her a quick hug and headed to her classroom.

Sarah swallowed. *Probably not.* She followed her students into her room. *Nick and I are finished.*

At lunch, Becca cornered her again. "Any word?"

Shaking her head, Sarah gave a deep sigh. "I'll call him on my off period."

Teachers lined their students up to return to their classrooms. Becca waved her hand for her class and gave Sarah a smile. "Quit worrying. Nick will fix it."

Wrong. They'd kept their past from Rachel. A past tainted by adult complications a ten-year-old wouldn't understand.

You can't fix that.

As soon as her last student left, she headed to the music office she shared with the band and orchestra director. Their department phone was perfect for private conversations unlike the one in the teachers' lounge where others could listen. She pressed Nick's number from her contact favorites. He picked up right away. "Why haven't you called. Is Rachel okay? She's not in school."

"Sorry. Things got crazy last night. Mara worked us in for a session this morning, so I let Rachel stay home. After our appointment, I walked into a major crisis on a job site when I got to work this morning."

They had needed to talk with their therapist. That did not bode well. "What happened?"

"It's complicated."

Sarah chewed on her lip waiting for him to explain more. A claxon blared in the background.

You have got to be kidding me. Not now.

"What's that siren? Is everything ok?"

"It's a fire drill bell. I can't stay in the building or be caught on my phone. Call me later, please."

"We need to talk in person. How 'bout we meet after your lessons? I'll stop by and pick you up, or we can meet at Feelin' Good. Your choice."

Sarah grinned for the first time that day. He wasn't taking her response for granted this time like he had the first time he surprised her with a dinner offer. "Pick up some burgers. My last student leaves at six. Becca has bunko tonight. We'll have the house to ourselves."

Sarah stood in her doorway watching Nick talk to her departing piano student. He was good with kids. Why was Rachel such a problem? What wasn't he telling her?

She stepped aside to let him in. "What happened when you and Rachel talked with Mara?"

Nick rubbed his finger across her forehead. "Hang on. I skipped lunch."

Sarah took his hand and pulled him into the living room. "We can eat after you tell me what happened.

"Can I at least remind you what I want? What I pray you want." He pulled her into his arms.

She slipped out of his grip. "This." She waved her hand between them. "This can't happen unless Rachel accepts us."

His eyes clouded with the doubt that was eating at her. "She will. She needs some time. I understand why Rachel reacted the way she did. I kinda glossed over some details when I told you Barb and I worked out a truce." He sighed. "When alcohol's involved, a real truce is next to impossible."

"But you said Barb joined AA."

"Joining and succeeding don't necessarily go hand in hand. Not that she didn't try. The addiction was stronger. Longest she lasted between drinks was almost a year. Usually less. Months. Sometimes weeks. Her episodes were horrible. Barb was not a kind drunk. Being caught in her cross-hairs was hell."

He stabbed his hand through his hair as if that could push the memories away and stared at the Christmas tree.

Sarah gathered his hand in hers. "I've seen the aftermath of an alcoholic parent's binges play out in my students. It's hard and those memories linger into adulthood."

"Al-Anon helps. Rachel comes with me to kid meetings, and we work with Mara, but sometimes, like the other night, those bad memories overpower everything."

"But she'd said she was fine with us being friends and excited about our date to your Christmas party."

"True. And I think she is. Unfortunately, she's spent years hearing her mother rail at me about still loving Miss Preacher Kid Pretty Princess, Barb's name for you, every time she got drunk. I spent those same years doing the best I could to convince Rachel I loved her mother. Seeing that ornament made everything Barb had said a reality. Truth. At least in Rachel's mind."

Sarah struggled to mask her growing fear she was about to lose everything again. "I'm not sure we can change Rachel's mind."

"We will. This morning was a start Mara helped me explain how you and I had dated in high school, and we were becoming good friends again. Mara stressed that didn't mean I quit loving Rachel or her mother. Same thing I'd told her." His eyes met Sarah's. "I already told you, the part about loving Barb wasn't the whole truth. I've always loved you. I'll never stop, but I did love Barb for giving me Rachel. Someday I'll explain all that to Rachel. Until then, I'm going to figure out a way to broker peace with her about us."

There would never be another man for Sarah either, but she loved him too much to force him to choose between her and his daughter.

"We need more than peace, Nick. I love you, I do, but Rachel has to accept me. It sounds like that's not going to happen. What was her reaction to what you and Mara said?"

"Not as good as I would have liked." The angst in his voice frightened her.

"Meaning?"

"She doesn't want to see you or talk to you again. No piano lessons. Removed from your class at school."

Sarah slapped her chest with a gasp. The reality of her fears filled her with the heart-ripping pain she'd vowed to never feel again.

Nick slipped his arm around her shoulder, tucked her close. "But that doesn't mean I can't ever make her understand that I can love both of you."

She pulled away. "How? When her mind's set, indoctrinated against me her whole life. Even if you could, it won't work."

As much as he wanted her, it wasn't enough. Never would be enough.

He reached for her again. "You're wrong. She'll change her mind."

"And if she doesn't? I won't play the wicked stepmother. I can't." Her last words ended on a whisper. Life wasn't ever going to let her have Nick's love. It was the cruelest of all jokes.

He stared at the Christmas tree for several long silent minutes as if he could find a rebuttal in the twinkling lights. They both knew there was no counterargument he could offer. His daughter had to be his priority. As she should be. That didn't make it hurt any less.

Sarah brushed the hair off his forehead. "When Rachel is ready, maybe we can try again. Until she is, you have to put your daughter first, Nick."

He rose slowly. Defeat slumped his shoulders. "I love you with all my heart and soul. I refuse to give up on us again."

"It's out of your hands."

The front door banged closed with a heart-shattering click behind him. His words should have brought joy, but the joy wasn't there. Only desperation. There was nothing more to say. They both had to put Rachel first, the child had suffered enough already. Sarah's tears fell unchecked.

Still, her hopeful heart prayed for a miracle. Prayed that somehow her soul wouldn't shatter. She could see this through.

But if Rachel couldn't stand to be with Sarah for a simple piano lesson, there was no way Sarah could be a part of their family. Even a miracle prayer couldn't change that terrible truth.

Chapter 15

Nick stormed to his truck and slapped his fist against the steering wheel. He couldn't get Sarah's words out of his head. How could she give up on them so easily?

Why wouldn't she? Hadn't that been what you did when you left her after Barb announced her pregnancy?

Anger wrestled with his need to convince Sarah she was wrong. But how?

Their conversation like a broken record cycled over and over in his head as he drove home. No matter how many times, he couldn't remember her ever saying she'd wait. Would she?

Panic swept through him as he tried to picture life without Sarah.

His phone interrupted the morbid thoughts. Ethan's name flashed on the car's navigation screen. Nick answered with Bluetooth. "Hey, pal. You're up early."

"Lining things up so I can be there for the Christmas party with the merger documents. How are things on your end?"

He slapped the steering wheel again. The Christmas party. In all the uproar, Nick had forgotten.

"Okay." Even he heard the lie in his voice.

"Why am I not convinced? What's happened?"

"I'm drowning. I don't know what I'm doing. I took a risk not telling Rachel about my past with Sarah. I was hoping she'd be so attached to Sarah when I did explain, it wouldn't matter. Bad call. Rachel found out and she's refusing to have anything to do with Sarah."

"Sounds like a setback but not unfixable."

"Afraid it is. Sarah's bailing on me."

"Impossible. That fouls up personal plans for both of us."

"Yeah, I know. I'm sorry, but Sarah sounded pretty firm that until Rachel was on board, *we* wouldn't happen. And, trust me, Rachel's pulling a major Barb. Reconciliation's not happening anytime soon."

"We just need to re-strategize. I'll leave as soon as I can. We must fix this."

"About that. Sarah doesn't know you're my partner. Yet."

"*Merde! Pourquoi pas?*" Nick was pretty sure that translated to why the flip not? Or maybe something worse. When Ethan mimicked his grand-père, he tended to forget Nick's French was pretty much nonexistent.

Ethan continued, "Secrets are what messed everything up in the first place. You didn't learn your lesson?"

"It's complicated. I didn't feel comfortable asking Sarah to keep your return a secret. That TPS thingy is still in full force. I couldn't be sure she would go along if I told her. I was planning to share everything at the Christmas party. Together we could have explained how you wanted to win back her sister. Now I'm not so sure we can."

"*Merde*! I may have to kill you if you've screwed this up."

"I wouldn't blame you." Because, without Sarah, Nick didn't know how to go on.

Sarah's bottom lip trembled as she watched Nick's truck pull away. Someday, he would understand and give up just like she had. Her heart of hearts knew she had done the right thing for all of them. She sank to the couch, clicked on the television hoping a dose of Hallmark movie happy endings would renew her faith in happy endings.

When Becca came home after Bunko, she found Sarah huddled with the Christmas throw pulled up to her chin and tears trailing silently down her cheeks.

"Oh, my god. What's wrong? These movies

aren't supposed to be sad." Becca dropped beside her. "Tell me."

"Rachel doesn't ever want to see me again." Sarah took a deep breath.

"Wait. What? What does that mean?"

"Rachel hates me. Nick's gone. Probably forever this time. If his daughter doesn't want me to be around, I'm not going to force him to choose between us."

"Aren't you giving up a little soon? Kids do change their minds."

"I'm not sure Rachel will. She's had years of Barb's poison. I'll always be the villain. Our lives would be miserable. I'll always love him, but I can't do that." Sarah tossed the throw aside, stood and swiped at her cheeks. *Enough of this pity-party.* "It is what it is. I'm going to bed."

Sarah felt Becca's eyes on the back of her neck following her down the hallway. "Don't give up," her twin called, her voice as unsure as Sarah felt.

Letting Nick go was the right thing to do. No matter the queasy, stabbing pain in her stomach, she refused to let the loss consume her. Life was still coming at her like a freight train. She had to keep it together. There were grades to get out, lessons to teach, the big Christmas program. She had to come up with a new finale now that Rachel wouldn't play.

Her gut flipped over as another tsunami of grief and anxiety washed over her. She turned on the shower, stepped inside, and let the warm water soothe her weary body. Tomorrow would be soon enough to deal with everything.

Tonight, she would try her best to let go of her dream.

Chapter 16

Sarah was good with her decision until Sundays loomed long and lonely without Nick, Rachel, and their board games.

Reality became real. And it hurt.

When she spotted the child at school, Rachel would look away. But not before Sarah saw the blame in her eyes. The child believed all the misery in her life was Sarah's fault. Rachel might never see her mother's alcohol addiction as the true cause. One day Sarah'd be at peace with all that.

Not today.

Today she missed Nick's smile. She missed them both. She yearned to call him to see how things were going with Rachel. Was she still playing her baby grand? Had Nick signed off on his merger with the French company?

As much as she wanted to know, she wouldn't accept his calls the way things were now. After the first few texts with declarations of his love and office party reminders, she'd stopped reading. She couldn't be second place in his heart. Rachel had to be on board or being together could never work.

With renewed determination, she refocused on finding a closing for the Christmas program. Playing a duet with Rachel had been so perfect.

Becca leaned her shoulder against Sarah's office doorframe. "Whatcha doing? Every time you disappear, I find you in here digging through old school Christmas programs and notes. Don't tell me you're organizing files. Something's wrong."

"You mean besides the obvious?" She held her hand up to stop Becca from answering. "My finale idea isn't going to work anymore either, and I can't seem to come up with a new one."

Becca's arms crossed. "Let me guess. Rachel was going to play."

Sarah nodded. No point in keeping it a secret now. "We were going to play a Christmas duet."

"That's a major bummer. I see why you're scrambling. There's always the old standby of Santa or an elf appearing."

"The best finales are ones where a student is involved. I have better attendance. Anticipating the surprise always draws everyone in. Another student wouldn't have enough time to prepare."

"Maybe Nick or Ms. Lorene could convince Rachel to at least do the Christmas program."

"I won't ask them. Even if she agreed, it'd give Nick false hope. I'll figure something out."

"If you say so, but he's living on that hope like it's his last breath."

Nick left Rachel at her classroom door and headed toward Sarah's room as he'd done every morning since Sarah called it quits.

Miss Nancy, the school secretary, had winked when he walked in with Rachel today. He'd easily talked her into letting him slip by the first time. She remembered him from his visits to the principal's office and how he and Sarah had once been a couple. She'd been willing to bend rules.

He was so pathetic, hanging outside Sarah's classroom to catch a glimpse of her. Something his teenage self had done often. But as an adult he still couldn't stop himself either. Sarah wasn't answering his calls or texts. He needed to talk to her. Convince her they belonged together.

He'd given in quietly before. Hadn't fought for her. They could have figured out a way to deal with Barb's pregnancy, provided for his child, and still been together. Back then, he'd been embarrassed, ashamed. He'd cheated on the preacher's daughter and cut out as fast as he could before he was tarred and feathered. He wasn't running again. He loved his daughter, but Sarah was his other half. He'd never be complete without her. He wasn't giving up this time.

His steps slowed as he neared her doorway. One of these times when she spotted him, she'd respond. Even though Becca warned him, saying TPS wasn't working. Becca's arguments on his behalf were falling on deaf ears too.

Maybe Sarah was right, a relationship was impossible, but he had to keep trying. His heart wouldn't let him do anything else.

Nick stood in Sarah's classroom doorway and waved. "Miss you" he mouthed when he wanted to shout, *I love you.*

Sarah gave him the *you're-a-moron* look she'd mastered in third grade. "Class, y'all hum your parts. I'll be right back."

She came toward him. His heart did flips. She didn't slam the door in his face. Instead, she clasped his forearm and pulled him out of the doorway. "This has got to stop. I'm not going anywhere with you until Rachel is okay with us. Certainly not your office party. Quit asking, please."

She turned heel and went back to her class, closing the door on him.

He refused to be disheartened by her words. She'd spoken to him for the first time in over a week. That counted as progress. Didn't it?

When he got home that evening, he heard voices coming from the kitchen. He took his time hanging up his coat and listened.

"You know exactly why he's so sad all the time." His mom's voice edged with frustration.

"But it's Christmas. He should be happy."

"He should. So should you. But you're not."

"I am."

"Really? I don't think so. You've stopped playing the piano. Your friend Catherine doesn't come over." He could see his mom's pursed lips, feel her hard stare at Rachel.

"I don't invite Catherine because I think it makes Dad think about how he doesn't have any friends."

"But he does. Sarah's his friend. If you don't want him to feel sad, maybe you need to rethink your behavior toward her."

"No!" Rachel's voice rose an octave.

"Young lady, don't take that tone with me. It's disrespectful."

Rachel had the grace to blush and hang her head. "Sorry, Granny."

"I love you, sweet girl. I don't like seeing my two favorite people so unhappy. It's just a suggestion, sweetheart."

And just like that, the belligerent kid was back. "I don't care. I won't be around her. Mom always said Miss Sarah was the reason Dad didn't love her."

Nick had heard enough. "I'm home. What are my two favorite girls up to?"

Rachel ran from the kitchen and lunged into his arms. "We're decorating cookies. Come help us."

"For Sarah's school program." His mom pointed

out. "Like I've made every year for her Christmas program since she started teaching."

Nick slid Rachel back to the ground. "And you're helping? Does that mean you've reconsidered going with us?"

Rachel scrunched her face. "No way. It's bad enough I have to be at the same school with her."

He didn't want Rachel launching on him like the last time he suggested the same thing. "Fine. I get you don't like Sarah right now. You don't have to go to her program. But whether I go or not is my choice. I'll take Mom and get a sitter to stay with you."

Rachel crossed her arms again. Tighter this time. "I don't need a sitter. I'll be eleven next month. I'm old enough to stay by myself."

"Well, you can't." He reached for a cookie. His mom brushed his hand away. "After you eat."

"Did you finish your homework? Your math teacher emailed that you haven't been turning in homework lately."

His mom lifted his dinner plate from the microwave. "I had her do it before we started the cookies. We put it in her backpack."

"Okay. Maybe..." He glanced at the kitchen clock. "Oops. I didn't realize how late is. Time for you to get ready for bed."

Rachel's nostrils flared. "I'm gonna be eleven soon. I shouldn't have to be in bed at nine."

"And when you are, we'll discuss it. Now go get ready for bed."

Tears filled her eyes. "You don't love me. You never want to spend time with me." Rachel ran from the room.

Nick shifted to stand. His mom stopped him. "Eat your dinner. I'll go."

Try as he might, dinner tasted like guilt and regret. The second hand on the kitchen clock echoed in the silence as minutes ticked, longer and longer.

What was taking his mom so long to put Rachel to bed? He stayed glued to the chair, pushing his food around.

"She's all settled," Mom said when she finally returned.

Nick set his utensils on his plate, rinsed both and loaded the dishwasher, then turned and leaned against the counter. "You were gone a long time. How was she?"

"Mad at you. Blaming Sarah."

"I'll go talk to her." She raised her hand palm out. "No. We talked. Let her stew. She was disrespectful to both of us. If you don't get a handle on it now, it's going to be out of control by the time she hits the real teen years. She'll be fine."

His mom was a smart woman, he would listen to her counsel. "She may be, but I might not."

"It's all going to work out. I heard Rachel playing Christmas carols when I came back from taking cookies next door to Miss Keta. Be sure to tell Mara that when you go tomorrow."

"Playing the piano? She hasn't done that since she stormed out of Sarah's. That's good."

"I agree." His mom walked over and gave him a hug. "Have a little faith. She's not Barb."

Chapter 17

Sitting in Mara's outer office, Nick flipped through a *Sports Illustrated* while he waited for Rachel. His eyes didn't register the words or pictures. He wanted to press his ear to the wall, to know what was being said behind that closed door. Since he hadn't been invited in this time, he prayed his daughter was talking about whatever she discussed with his mom. Rachel's attitude had seemed better these last few days.

She'd only been inside a short time when the door opened. Rachel plopped into the chair he left. He searched her eyes for a hint of how things had gone. Steel stared back at him. No softening. Nothing. His hopes dashed.

"Your turn." Mara motioned him inside.

"I'll be right back."

Mara closed the door and sat in the chair across from him. "How are you holding up?"

"Disappointed. Mom said she'd heard Rachel playing Christmas carols. I thought that meant she might be changing her mind." He tilted his head toward the door. "Didn't look like it from the expression on her face."

"Rachel guards her feelings better than most adults. Behind that hard exterior, things are working. We talked about how miserable you are and why you were. I do think she's listening."

"Could you maybe talk to Sarah, convince her?"

Mara laughed. "Sarah's not my patient. You are." With that, she started those touchy-feeling questions he'd come to hate.

He related how Sarah shooed him away from her classroom door, telling him not to contact her again. "At least she spoke to me and didn't just slam the door in my face like before. That's progress, right?"

"As your friend, I can say yes. As your therapist, I'd say don't count heavily on a fast reconciliation. Sarah's got a lot of hurt hanging on."

Nick dropped his head. "I know. I want to make it up to her if she'd just let me."

"Rachel and Sarah have a lot in common besides loving you. They will both come around. I can almost guarantee it." A soft bell chimed. "That's my next patient. I'll see y'all next week."

Guarantee it?

How could she be positive when everything seemed bleaker than ever? Was she just giving him a platitude because he couldn't take anymore despair?

"Will we see you at the school program?"

"Absolutely. It's Cody's favorite part of Christmas." She smiled at the mention of her son. Someday Nick was going to be brave enough to ask what happened to Cody's father.

Someday, when he got his own life straightened out.

"I'm getting a sitter for Rachel and taking Mom. See you there."

"Rachel told me. That was a very good move on your part."

The bell sounded again. Mara walked him to the door. "See you next time."

That evening Rachel bolted to her room after supper and refused to come out. Nick knocked on her door. "We're leaving. Are you sure you don't want to come with us?"

Nothing. No response.

Well, that's her choice. His was to support his mom and Sarah. "We'll see you later."

After Nick gave instructions to the sitter, he helped his mom with her coat.

She handed him her keys. "Let's take mine. Please. It takes a pole vaulter to get in and out of that truck of yours."

He laughed. "Sarah says the same thing." His smile drifted away. *Or did.*

At the school, he dropped his mom at the door and parked. Pastor Fitz waited for him when he returned. "Full house tonight. There's always a big crowd for Sarah's Christmas programs." Fatherly pride thickened in his voice. "We saved seats up front for you and Lorene."

Nick fell in step beside him. "Thanks."

"I know this is a challenge. Your eyes give you away. I know your heart's broken. We appreciate how you are still supporting Sarah. We miss seeing you at Sunday lunches." Pastor Fitz squeezed his shoulder.

"And I miss hanging with the family. Unfortunately, Rachel is not giving in." Nick exhaled a hefty sigh. "And neither is your daughter."

"Girls can be pretty stubborn. That's why I was so happy with you and Ethan. We knew the twins had met their equals. You're back fighting for Sarah. Not sure what will happen with Becca. Don't think there will ever be any one but Ethan for her. Faith's the one who worries us. I'm not sure there's a man out there that can handle that one."

"That's what I tell myself about my Rachel."

"Faith's determined to be a lawyer and won't lift her head out of those books long enough to see life's passing her by. The twins are different. Their hearts desire has always been a home and family of their own."

Nick bit his tongue to keep from saying that was exactly what he and Ethan wanted. Another chance for a home and family with the pastor's twin daughters was the reason they'd both returned. But Nick couldn't share, not yet, even if it meant soothing the Pastor's unease. If Sarah didn't take

Nick back, Becca and Ethan might never have their chance.

They reached their seats on the front row. Nick gave Ms. Pat a hug and slipped around her to sit next to his mom. The gym lights flickered, and the chattering crowd quieted as Sarah guided the kids onto risers.

She wore a forest green velvet dress with a skirt that had a slit to her calf. Her hair glistened in an updo secured with a sequined clip. She looked professional. Sexy. His determination to win her back bubbled like oil when the drill struck a crude vein.

"Welcome everyone to our annual Christmas Program." Pivoting to the choir, Sarah raised her hands. Forty minutes later, she bowed and swept her hand toward the kids as applause rose. The crowd stood.

"What? No surprise this year?" Nick heard his mom ask Ms. Pat.

"I guess not," Sarah's mom answered.

"Tradition." His mom filled in for him. "Sarah always has a surprise ending for the Christmas program. With all that's gone on, she must be skipping it this year."

Rachel's friend Catherine stepped from the risers with a bouquet in her hand. Becca stopped her. "Hold up on the flowers for a sec, Catherine. Everyone please be seated."

Becca wiggled a come-hither finger toward Sarah. "We have a special guest for you this year.

Our Christmas surprise for you."

Nick shot a questioning glance to Pastor Fitz, who shrugged.

Becca took the microphone from a stunned Sarah. "Tonight, we will all have a very special treat."

Several teachers pushed the piano in front of the risers. Becca motioned toward the curtain behind the students. "We're ready now."

Rachel came forward, took Sarah's hand in hers, and pulled her down to say something in her ear.

Nick's mother gasped. "Oh, my."

Nick twisted his hands in his lap as the two women he loved whispered for what seemed like forever. Finally, Sarah smiled and gave his daughter a hug.

Becca gave the microphone to Rachel. She lifted the microphone to her lips. "This is a Christmas present for my dad that Miss Sarah and I planned before I backed out on her. I've changed my mind and Miss Sarah is willing to help me. Merry Christmas, Dad."

Rachel returned the microphone to Becca. She and Sarah walked to the piano. The bench screeched as they pulled it out. They whispered some more as Rachel set sheet music on the piano music rack.

The room went silent in anticipation.

"And now ladies and gentlemen, enjoy "Cantique de Noël." Becca swooped her hand toward them.

The two girls' fingers danced across the keys. Nick's mind raced with visions of Christmases that could be in their future. He thought his heart would explode.

The last note sounded. The gym erupted in a roar of whistles and applause. As the two stood to bow, Nick pushed his way through the crowd.

He circled his daughter and Sarah in his arms and swallowed back the unmanly tears of happiness gathering. "Best Christmas present ever."

Becca tapped his back. "We're going to our folks' house for hot chocolate and your mother's cookies. Join us."

Nick glanced from Sarah to Rachel. "Shall we?"

Both nodded.

Sarah slipped out from under his arm, stood on tiptoes, and kissed his cheek. "I'll go with Becca. Rachel will explain. See you there."

"What changed your mind?" Nick asked his daughter as soon as they were in his mom's car.

"Granny did," she said quietly from the backseat. "She told me how her dad had yelled ugly things at her and her mom when he'd been drinking. Things she still remembers."

Nick shot a questioning look his mom's way. "Granddad drank? You never told me."

"I don't like to talk about it." She tapped her purse on her lap. A tell for how hard the conversation was for her. "But Rachel needed to hear the story and know we don't have to let those words play in our heads forever. That they aren't the whole truth. We can choose to remember the good things instead."

"When I saw Ms. Mara this morning, I asked her why she didn't tell me that."

Nick wondered the same thing. Mara probably had, but not with the authenticity of his mom's words. "What'd she say?"

"That Granny's were sometimes wiser than therapists."

He reached over and squeezed his mom's hand. He'd thank her properly later.

Sarah met them at the door of her parents' house. "Better hurry before the cookies are all gone."

Rachel darted past them. "Those boys better not have eaten all of them."

Sarah turned to follow her. Nick held her back. "We need to talk."

"Let me get a jacket." She shivered. "It's cold out here."

Nick slid his jacket off and wrapped it around her shoulders. "I think I can keep you warm." He guided her to the porch swing. A pregnant silence swayed with them.

"What made her change her mind?" Sarah whispered.

"Mom. She talked to her while they were frosting your cookies. I'm not sure exactly what she said, but it stuck. I owe her big time."

She burrowed her face against his throat. "We both do."

He lifted her chin with his finger. First, he kissed the tip of her nose, then her eyes, and, finally, he claimed her soft mouth.

Afterward, his gaze locked with Sarah's. "Now will you come to my office party?"

She hesitated. Nick thought surely his chest would cave in from holding his breath. Finally, she gave his hand a squeeze and flashed a smile that danced in her eyes. "Can't wait. Will I get to meet your partner?"

A tingle went up his spine. Nick swallowed. "He'll be there."

And I pray you don't freak when you see that it's Ethan.

Chapter 18

Headlights flashed across the front sidelight windows as Nick's car turned into Sarah's driveway.

"Your chariot has arrived." Giggling, Becca pulled her twin away from the glass. "Can you believe we're watching like we used to on date nights?"

Sarah pulled her coat from the closet. "Truthfully, no." *But I do feel guilty that I have Nick back and you still have no one. It doesn't seem fair.*

Becca opened the door before Nick knocked. "She's ready."

Nick stepped inside. His head-to-toe perusal produced a voiceless *wow* followed by an approving grin that emphasized his cheekbones.

She and Becca had spent hours shopping for the perfect dress. They found paydirt the minute they spotted the soft red silk dress with a ruched bodice ending in a tuck at the side.

Returning his smile, Sarah tapped his bowtie. "Not so bad yourself."

Becca hugged her sister. "Make the night magic. Both of you."

Nick guided Sarah toward the door. As Becca closed the door, he winked hew way and patted his pants pocket. "I plan to."

"Your mother's car?" Sarah slid into the sedan. "I'm so glad I won't have to pole-vault into your truck in this dress."

"Mom says the same thing. That's why she insisted I drive her car. Rachel asked if we would go by my house for quick pictures. She wants to see your dress and take some selfies." He leaned on the doorframe. "We don't have to. It's totally up to you."

Rachel wanted to see her dress. Maybe I've finally won the girl over.

Sarah and Nick posed in front of the grand piano in his mom's living room. Rachel clicked a few shots with his phone. Ms. Lorene waved her Nikon camera. "I want some of you all together." She signaled her granddaughter to join them.

Rachel gave a sweet little smile, though she didn't move. She bit her lip, glancing at Sarah. Her eyes remained laced with wariness.

"Our fresh start, remember?" Sarah extended her hand.

Ms. Lorene's camera clicked several times. "One more, this time with you and Sarah on the bench. I didn't have my camera the other night."

"Last one. We don't want to be late," Nick cautioned.

Sitting at the keyboard, the temptation to play their duet was too great. Sarah gave Rachel a nod, and they did a hurried rendition of "Cantique de Noël."

Ms. Lorene clapped. Nick pointed to his watch. "Okay. Now we really do *have* to go."

"Where's the party?" Sarah asked when they pulled out of the driveway.

"Downtown Houston," He swallowed hard. "Unfortunately, we're going to have to head straight there."

"Were we going someplace else first?"

"I had a plan, if we'd had time. But it's fine. Hearing you and Rachel play was wonderful."

"She's going to make a great pianist." Sarah smoothed her dress.

"Are you nervous?"

"A little, and excited. This *is* my first office party with you."

"Be yourself. Everyone will love you like I do."

I hope he's right. The business world is foreign territory for me.

Butterflies, worse than any she'd ever experienced when performing, knocked against Sarah's chest when Nick pulled into the porte-cochere of the expensive hotel she'd only seen in pictures. "Your office party is here?"

"Uh-huh. At my new partner's penthouse." Nick slid from the car when the valet opened his door.

Sarah climbed out her open door. *I can't wait to meet this man.*

Nick slid her arm over his and guided her through the glass doors into the tiny, but ornate entryway lobby. Gold gild sparkled in the ceiling from the crystal chandeliers. Her heels clicked on the black-veined marble floor. The butterflies started to do somersaults.

"Good evening, Mr. Stevens." The elevator attendant waved through the open doors.

"Penthouse, please," Nick said as though he'd done it a million times before.

The elevator doors opened into a chrome and glass, ultra-contemporary living area. Nick slid her coat from her shoulders. The attendant waiting inside the doorway whisked it away, draped over his arm.

Nick ushered her toward the open balcony doorway where a man, watching their progress, stood in the shadows. He looked up as Nick guided her into the crowd. *Nick's partner?*

The mixed scent of perfume and aftershave blended with a cloud of cigar smoke and outdoor heater exhaust that had drifted inside from the open balcony door. Sarah's head swam as Nick introduced her to guests who stopped them along the way to the balcony.

She felt like she'd been dropped into an alternate universe. Definitely not her schoolteacher world. Christmas parties in the teacher's lounge were never like this. The butterflies felt more like a boulder avalanche as she tried to make sense of a scene she'd never imagined.

At last, they reached the balcony. "Sarah." The man took her shoulders and air-kissed both cheeks.

The voice, the face, both were familiar but at the same time not. Pulling back, she stared. Her mouth dropped open. "Ethan? Ethan Wells?"

"No, it's LaMott now."

Her gaze flew from Ethan to Nick. "I'm confused. What are you doing here?"

"Ethan's my new partner." Nick's smile faltered.

Anger replaced the torrent of butterflies in Sarah's gut. *How could he forget to share that little detail?*

"Why didn't you tell me?"

Ethan answered before Nick had a chance. "I asked him not to."

"Why not?"

"I wanted to talk to you before he told you," Ethan answered.

"So, talk. Where have you been?"

"It's a long story." Ethan sighed. "A not so pretty story. Not one for tonight." Ethan took her hands. "Tonight, I need to ask for your help."

She jerked her hands away, slapped her crossed arms to her chest. "You're both out of your minds. Why would I help either of you? I'm calling Becca right now."

"No. Wait." Ethan leaned back and gripped the balcony railing at his sides. His eyes held steady with hers. "I left because I was kidnapped."

"What?"

"Turns out I had a family in Paris I didn't know about. They came and got me that day."

"And, in the last ten plus years you couldn't find a way to let Becca know? To let any of us know. Why not?"

"I tried at first. Believe me, it was all I could think about. But I was forced to give up. Until now."

Nick stepped between them. "It's true. When you meet his Grand-père, you'll understand completely."

Sarah's chin rose. "If Ethan truly loved Becca, he would have found a way."

"He has. And Ethan's the reason I could come back," Nick said.

"It's complicated." Ethan's eyes pleaded. "I promise you'll know everything."

"When? This is some wild cockamamie story you're telling me. Another family? What kind of family kidnaps you then keeps you from the one person you said you loved? How am I supposed to believe a word you say?"

"I will tell you what you want to know. Not now though. I believe your sister deserves to hear it first...from me."

"Oh no you don't! You've got to explain to me before I'll allow you anywhere near my sister. I won't let you break her heart again."

"I've never stopped loving your sister. I'm not going to hurt her. I know this sounds unbelievable, but it's the truth." Ethan closed his eyes, took a deep breath, and exhaled. "I don't blame you. I wouldn't believe me either, but the thing is, I must go back to Paris for Christmas. I only came over because Nick and I needed to announce our merger. I'll explain to Becca, to everyone, when I return. It won't be long. Please put that TPS thing on hold and promise me you won't say anything until I do."

Nick's gaze locked with hers. "Please. Give him a chance like you did me."

"I... I don't know." Her resolve wavered. *Nick stayed with Barb because of Rachel. Maybe Ethan's reasons are legitimate too. Can I trust him a little while longer?*

Ethan continued, "I know you want to protect your sister, but please, I'm begging. We don't want to blow your chance for the twin wedding you two always talked about."

"Protect my sister? You have no idea what I'm willing to do. If you step out of line or—" *Twin wedding? What did Ethan mean?* Sarah shot Nick a questioning look. "Don't we have to be engaged first?"

"*Merde!* He hasn't asked you yet?" Ethan shot Nick a disgusted glare.

Nick fidgeted, breaking eye contact. "My plan fell apart...we took longer at Mom's than I thought..."

"Then what are you waiting for? Get on with it. I'll go tend to our guests." With a flick of his wrist, Ethan disappeared into the crowd.

Sarah placed a hand on her popped hip. "You had a plan?"

"I did. I was going to stop by the stadium where I first proposed, but with your duet replay at Mom's there wasn't time."

"You're saying it's my fault?" She jacked an eyebrow.

His cheeks flushed. "No that's not what I meant. I just… I wanted my proposal to be special…something you'd remember."

"Well, look at this." She swept her hand out to the building's lit with holiday lights. "The Houston skyline decked for Christmas and stars twinkling, how could anything be more special?"

"Right." Nick dropped to his knees and flipped open a telltale black box. "Sarah Fitzpatrick, will you marry me?"

How long had she waited to hear that question from him again? And to know that Ethan would be asking Becca. It was more than special, it was perfect.

Sarah tugged him against her. "Yes. Yes. Yes." She kissed him. "But no wedding until Ethan convinces Becca to marry him."

"Seriously?"

She admired her ring. "Seriously. Becca and I have wanted a twin wedding forever. And, if Ethan's telling the truth, he can win her back and our dream will be reality."

"I'll hate every second, but I can wait. But you have to help Ethan as much as Becca helped me."

"Becca helped you?"

"She did. She believes, like I do, we belong together."

Ethan and Becca do belong together, same as Nick and me. "Can you promise she won't get hurt again?"

"Ethan has nothing but the best intentions for Becca. He loves her. Always has."

Sighing, Sarah rolled her shoulders. "This is so strange, and I don't even know the whole story."

"But you know me. You trust me, right?"

"With all my heart." He may have kept Ethan's existence a secret, but she did trust him. He would protect Becca too.

"Then believe me when I say, with your help, Ethan's going to convince Becca. You two will have your twin wedding."

"Well, that makes my decision easy, I promise. TPS to the rescue." She winked.

Author's Note

Dear Reader,

Thank you so much for reading *When Love Endures*. If you'd like to make sure you never miss a new release, sign up for my newsletter at https://judythemorgan.com/ and please like my Facebook page at https://www.facebook.com/JudytheMorgan/

Word of mouth is incredibly important for helping other readers discover new authors.

If you enjoyed Sarah and Nick's story, please help others find and enjoy the book, too. Write a review and post on GoodReads or Amazon to tell others why you liked this book. I appreciate any and all reviews (whether positive or negative or somewhere in between).

Recommend the book to friends, readers' groups, and discussion boards so other readers can find it. Discussion questions for book clubs are available upon request.

Until next time!
Judythe

About the Author

Judythe Morgan was an Army brat then Army wife which means she's traveled a lot. She's been a teacher, an antiques dealer, former mayor's wife, and sometimes-church pianist. Mommy to an Old English sheepdog named Finnegan MacCool and a Maltese named Buster, there's always a wild adventure brewing.

Her diverse experiences make her life full, her characters vivid, and her stories authentic and award-winning. Besides fiction, she writes a weekly blog at www.judythewriter.com

Sign up for her free newsletter to keep up with her latest news and subscriber-only sneak peaks:

https://judythemorgan.com/

OTHER TITLES IN THIS INSPIRATIONAL SERIES:

When Love Blooms – Andy & Darcy

AND, COMING SOON:

When Love Returns – Becca & Ethan
When Love Trusts – Josh & Mara
When Love Concedes – Faith
When Love Surprises – Sammy

Also by Judythe

Seeing Clearly

Ex-cop Dawson McKey is consumed by revenge after a cartel's bomb kills his twin sons. He trusts no one and vows payback. He refuses to get close to anyone, let alone fall in love again. But widow Evie Parker challenges his thinking. She's raising her grandson after her only child and his wife die in a suspicious car accident and it's taking a toll.

Alarms go off in Dawson's head when Evie receives threatening emails concerning her grandson. Then Evie's nanny disappears with her grandson. Dawson knows something is deadly wrong.

Pushed to their limits searching for the toddler, will Dawson and Evie learn seeing clearly is the only way to live and love?

Claiming Annie's Heart

An Irish Love Story

Annie Foster stays in Ireland after boarding school to nanny a widower's infant daughter. Five years later, the widower proposes.

Her first love Chad Jones, whom she believes abandoned her, arrives weeks before the wedding on an undercover assignment probing her fiancé's connection with IRA terrorists. Chad's determined to change Annie's mind and her heart because he's never stopped loving her.

Which man will claim Annie's heart?

The Promises Series

Two men and one woman met at Eighth Army Headquarters, South Korea in the turbulent Vietnam War years and found their lives linked together forever. The PROMISES series chronicles the life and loves of Lily Reed, Alex Cabot, and David Sands. Each sequel is a standalone novel.

Book 1, Love in the Morning Calm

Book 2, The Pendant's Promise

Book 3, Until He Returns

Book 4, Promises to Keep